D1596059

Little Nothing
Dee Holloway
Copyright © 2023 by Dee Holloway

ISBN
979-8-9867543-4-5

Library of Congress Control Number
9798986754345

Queen of Swords Press LLC
Minneapolis, MN
www.queenofswordpress.com
Published in the United States

Cover Design by Caitlin Cadieux.
Interior Design by Terry Roy of Teryvisions.

Little Nothing

DEE HOLLOWAY

CONTENTS

ACKNOWLEDGMENTS

To MOLLY AND TARA, first readers always, my thanks for your enthusiasm and understanding. A thousand thanks also to Catherine and Queen of Swords, for finding Bess and Jonnie a home. To Caitlin, whose art reveals what's inside my head—there is no one like you. To Christa, my Florida lifer, and to all the moss-draped paths we haven't explored yet.

To every writer of horse books for weird little girls, I owe you the world.

INTRODUCTION

BEGAN BESS AND JONNIE's story in 2019, a Camp
NaNoWriMo project that spun out of a short piece
whose chief charms were atmospheric. Inside that
short piece, it seemed, were characters longing for more
life, worthy of closer study: two girls who might elucidate
what I loved most about my troubled home state, Florida;
two girls who might exorcise some of the demons atten-
dant to growing toward queerness in Florida.

In 2023, Florida life is even more fraught—rife with
attacks on higher education, book challenges, and trans-
phobic legislation—and its environment even more fragile
than when I was a child. My hometown lies at sea level; it
seems likely to change dramatically, perhaps even disap-
pear, in my lifetime. Florida's waterways, the heart of its
unique character bubbling out through limestone veins,
are at highest risk. Its ocean and Gulf, its vast St. Johns
River and vaster Lake Okeechobee, its cold springs, its vital
mingling of salt and fresh in marshes and wetlands: its

easiest sell, in tourist terms, comes cheapest for law-makers and corporations alike. The devil's main temptation these days is to give into despair.

Yet since I was young, first reading *The Yearling* and then *Their Eyes Were Watching God, The Yonahlossee Riding Camp for Girls, Made for Love, Milk Blood Heat,* books by Sarah Gerard and Lauren Groff and Erin Slaughter and Joe Fletcher and Linda Buckmaster, I believed my state was worthy of art and representation on the page. I write frantically against its demise by climate change or political destruction, general apathy or targeted, venomous mockery. I write most specifically in hopes of capturing the magic in its water, the texture and sorrow of its history, of fracturing the neon façade. Bess and Jonnie's story is an old one, maybe not one readers expect to find in the swampy wilds—beauty and devotion on the frontier, Black horsewomen and spellbinding seamstresses, sapphic love in a time of utmost human cruelty, joy found in strange beasts and the oft-othered self. It's never been difficult for me to believe magic lives in the Florida landscape. I've always hoped to convince others of the possibility the state holds—for restitution, for progress—even on its current path.

The best salve for the deepest wounds is to love openly.

Dee Holloway
April 2023
Schenectady, New York

LITTLE NOTHING

CHAPTER ONE

*I*T WAS MARKET DAY, and Jonnie had bled through her best shirt.

She hissed as I drew the shirt over her head, turning slightly so that I could see the gash running cockeyed over her ribs. There was a bandage on it, but whoever had put it on had done a poor job. She swore when I touched the edge, where blood welled beneath the cloth.

"Well, if you'd just let me do it in the first place—" My fingers were gentler than my words. I unwound the stained cotton from her side and dropped it on the hay scattered in the back of the wagon. "Who tied this up, Keke? Somebody else with hooves instead of hands?"

"Bess," she said, almost a whine. I kissed her cheek to keep her distracted while I swabbed the wound with water from a flask Ma passed me. "Lord a'mercy, this couldn't have waited?"

"Waited 'til what? You fainted right off the cart here? You already ruined your nice shirt." I folded the afore-mentioned shirt twice and pressed it to her side, so that part of it covered her chest and part of it the gash. "Here. Hold this. Press it down hard."

"I know how to dress a wound," she muttered, but she did what I said. I heard Pa snicker above our wagon horse's hoofbeats. "What am I supposed to wear then, Miss Fix-It?"

I didn't have an answer for that, though we'd need to come up with something and right quick. The market town that served Sawgrass was but fifteen miles north and we were nearly there. She couldn't go sauntering through the stalls and tip her hat to the church ladies with her bosoms out to the world. I was the only lucky soul who got to admire those bosoms. But we had more urgent matters just then, because if the bite in her side wasn't seen to, she wouldn't be sauntering anywhere at all.

Not to mention Jonnie'd think it a poor display of her expertise if word went around the limerunners she trained up so nice were still liable to bite—her or anyone else.

"Who gave you this anyway?" The sound of my voice would act as an anchor, and the question would force her mind to focus. I glanced at the boy trotting behind the wagon on his placid marsh-tackie, mounted to the side of the six limerunners following us in a string to market. The solid ponies were better at herding half-broke limeys than any dog. "That nasty blue-eyed one there? I'll bet it was him."

"Not him, Bess!" Aaron, Pa's horse-boy, piped from my left. He winked his own blue eyes, one and then the other, and lifted his hat toward the limey my joke had been aimed at. A single icy eye glared out of a white blaze scarring the colt's otherwise-inky coat. "She was out 'fore light in Sanctus River to catch a few more."

"Is that right," I said, not at all a question, and tugged the linen strip in my hand just a little tighter than necessary. It wound around Jonnie's ribs once and again, tucked beneath itself at intervals to form a basic plait. Her heart thudded under my palm, too fast and fluttering. "And how'd that go for you, Jonnie?"

She didn't answer, just pressed her lips together and stared hard at the clear sky above us.

WE'D PLANNED TO RIDE to market with six half-broke limeys, and so we'd proceeded, which meant that she hadn't managed to catch any extra. Keke, the trained beast trotting in her own string, belonged to Jonnie and would never be sold. Six were what she and Pa had agreed on with a few people looking to buy, and so why she'd needed to go out and try to haul in a couple more…

I pictured it: Jonnie in the shallows of the river, water to her hips and stock-still in the gray dawn. No one knew why dawn and dusk were the best time for catching limeys, no more than we knew why the fish bit during a downpour. Folk understood little better how their lives went—the mysterious way they spawned in Florida's brackish wetlands like tadpoles, then clambered to land like frogs. They could swim like gators and trot like any old pony. They were hard to track on dirt, near impossible in the water. All their lives the water called to them, seeped from them, turned their gaits fluid and their eyes cloudy. Their hides retained a slickness, their snake-necks a glimmer of gills no longer quite used for breath. Their bones lay close to their skins like the limestone from which they rose. The strangeness of them prompted most folk to call them the devil's own steeds, and lured a few, like Jonnie, close enough to—

Well, to bite.

I'd seen her rope the vicious water horses and drag them ashore, and I'd seen them bolt for deep water or the dense undergrowth of mangroves and marsh before she could lay hands on them. I'd seen a human body and a limey collide more times than I cared to.

Her arms grappling with the horse's head, and its predator's teeth sinking into her ribs. Limeys didn't have much mane to cling to; they were wily as eels and twice as mean, and every bit of them was a weapon.

I sighed and knotted the linen at the back, above the smooth dip of Jonnie's waist. Anyone else would've just tucked the ends in snug, but I left a torn strip loose, long enough to tie a particular way. *Sun for day and moon for night, bind this wound nice and tight.* It was a little nothing Jonnie's mother Maria had taught me, one of the litany of blessings and curses that lived in me far more deeply than anything I'd learned in church. Some of them had come down the peninsula with Maria after she'd escaped a Carolina plantation, from the western shores of Africa before that; some were French-Carib chants from the Maroons along the Lake of Spirits; some I believed Maria had woven herself, singing them to me and Jonnie as she braided our hair. Maria wouldn't be surprised when we got home and she heard I'd had cause to use it on her daughter.

My mother's voice rose above the hoofbeats. "I'm meaning to carry some of your old things to the church ladies, Bess. For the orphans. But they can spare a shirt, I'm sure, to another soul in need."

Ma's eyes creased with stifled laughter as Jonnie gingerly tugged the shirt over her head. I pulled the hem of her trousers up to the shirt's tail while she twitched her shoulders.

"Quite fine," Ma said, all serious, and this time Pa laughed outright. Ma shook her head, one hand clasping her hat in place. "Why didn't you tell us earlier, Jonnie?"

"I figured it'd be all right." She glanced at me, her dark eyes rolling. "I been bit before."

If that wasn't the truth.

"Well," I said, "you're washing that shirt yourself. I bet you can't get the bloodstains out."

"What do you bet?"

"Five cents' worth of candy from Mr. Lawrence's store."

"Or something sweeter," Jonnie said, a bit of smile touching her lips. She kissed my cheek, exactly where I'd kissed hers a few moments before, and heat wriggled in my belly. Aaron laughed at us from his pony, but I didn't care. The sun was out with no sign of summer storms, and the market lay just ahead, a scrawl of bright tents and wagons and the wood-shingled roofs of stores in town. We had wares to sell and money to spend and warmth had come back into Jonnie's face. Her cheeks filled up with their usual golden-brown hue instead of the ashen tone of pain and blood loss. The morning was good again.

"Thank you for taking care of me, Bess." Her hand curled into mine and she placed both of them on her knee, her brown fingers knobby and long and mine paler, dimpled. "Good thing you did, else I wouldn't have been fit to ride later."

I snorted. "Like I could've stopped you one way or the other."

Races were always the most popular feature of any market day. There was even a little ring between Sawgrass and the market town of Sawyer, a dirt oval pounded by horses' hooves, warmbloods and limeys alike. Grudges were settled on the track, and breeders' prides tested, but mostly people came to see the limeys run, to drink and bet whether blood would be spilled on the dirt that afternoon—and whether that blood would be human.

I sent up a quick prayer that Jonnie would come out of the races whole. She'd already sacrificed a pint of blood to limeys today.

The wagon drew up in our usual spot far to the back of the livestock tents where the limeys would be corralled and prevented from savaging people who came to gawk. Every market in our parts had a special round barn dug with ditches inside for the limeys to wallow; it kept their coats slick and seemed to sweeten their temperaments. While Ma unhitched our horse, Pa came around to help Jonnie and Aaron herd the water horses into their temporary home. That left me to gather the rest of our gear: the bundle of worn clothing Ma had mentioned was due to the Methodist ladies for charity, and jars of honey from the beehives Pa kept behind our inn, their pale gold syrup flavored with oak and orange blossoms.

The market crowded into my eyes and ears as I stood in the midst of it, turning slowly to take in each detail. Some sights were familiar, like the white steeple the Methodists had finally fundraised onto the top of their old pine-plank church and the faces of the people who lived in Sawyer mingled with those who'd come in, like us, from Sawgrass. But there was always something new to look at too, whether it was a baby who hadn't been born the last market day, or Missy Sawyer, the mayor's granddaughter, boasting a hat trimmed in brilliantly-dyed gull's feathers, or strange faces lounging on the fence encircling hogs for sale.

One of those new faces looked at me, a long look that cut through the crowd like a Bowie knife.

Between people moving across the square I caught glimpses of a military uniform, which meant he'd come from the fort at the coast or the garrison down the river from Sawgrass. Either way I didn't want his eyes on me, for no good came of military men. People in Sawgrass kept well away from the garrison, not least because most of us weren't quite on the right side of the law to begin with, and every girl had heard tales of what men with a bit of power believed they could do with it.

A hand slipped into mine, and Ma smiled down at me, her hat casting a shadow across her face. "Now that the beasts are settled, shall we take a turn about the doin's?"

The festive air of the town during a market day began to sink into my blood, driving away any lingering gloom. I looked once more at the hog pen, thinking that the uniform looked somewhat different from the ones I was used to, and then the man wearing it slipped from my mind entirely.

The sun was near sunk in the marshland to Sawyer's west when people began trickling over to the dirt track where horses were drawn up. By the look of it, the first race planned was for warmbloods, saddle horses and Arabian mixed-breeds and any four-legged thing a man cared to race against his fellows that hadn't been born in rivers or chilly springs.

"I like that gray," Jonnie said. She wriggled onto the fence some enterprising soul had built to stretch halfway around the oval, then pulled me up next to her. Someone elbowed me but I stayed put, my bottom firmly plumped on the pine slats. Jonnie kept her arm through mine and continued, "Look at that behind on him. Looks like a locomotive."

"That the kind of behind you like?" I said, pushing my hip against hers, and she giggled. "Well, I'd say you're not the only one. Just the other day I went out to fill up the trough when Aaron and Pa were busy with the limeys, and who do you think I saw in the barn staring at Jamie Little's chestnut like the thing had ribbons in his mane and frilly drawers?"

Jamie Little was a trapper who worked the area between Sawgrass and the coast, and his chestnut was unfriendly at best.

Jonnie laughed again, her eyes combing over the horses as their riders began lining them up. "Let's see. Was it the priest?"

I squealed. Surely Father Bartolome in his little church wasn't that lonely.

"Nah," Jonnie said, "I know who you mean, and lily-cheeked bastards don't deserve a horse like that." She spat into the dirt below our feet. "You're rich enough to buy a good horse, or smart enough to steal one, and if you're neither?"

She didn't have much use for boys like Warren Almquist, the tow-headed son of Sawgrass's miller, a shiftless good-for-naught I'd seen skulking around our barn one too many times.

"Point being," Jonnie said. "An animal built like that gray, why, they'll go forever."

I pondered this while the men riding the race got situated. I had more knowledge of horses than I really cared to, seeing as Jonnie was in love with anything on four hooves, though most of the inn's extra money came from limerunners and there wasn't a limey born built like the gray standing still as a statue twenty yards from where we sat. Far as I'd heard, this race was a dash, once around the dirt loop and whoever returned first to the starting post won. Distance didn't have much to do with it, only speed.

"So why are you betting on a horse that'll go forever when he only needs to come right back here?"

Jonnie grinned and tipped her cheek against mine. Our hat brims nudged one another. "I said I liked him, not that I was betting on him. Hey, Miz Marshall!"

The woman coming along the fence paused. She was dressed fine, more so than any of the other women out for the market and the races, and I admired her gown's green stripes. It was fitted in the latest style, or the latest to reach our part of the landscape at any rate; surely up in New York City and Richmond they'd already moved on, but Miz Marshall looked very modish in her pagoda sleeves and tatted lace collar. Not a droplet of sweat marred her cheek, and beneath her straw bonnet thick auburn hair was massed in smooth braids.

I touched my own braids, tucking a loose tail back into its woven knot.

"And how can I help you today, Miss Johanna?" Miz Marshall smiled. Her blue eyes were sharp as heron beaks. "Miss Elizabeth. How are your parents?"

"Just fine." Some people—the Methodist ladies, mostly—thought being polite to Miz Marshall wasn't necessary, but I liked her. All right, maybe I was a little afraid of her, or maybe I wondered how I could be like her, someday. Said parents had raised me to be polite in the meantime. "Thank you, ma'am."

"Five dollars on the bay gelding, Miz Marshall," said Jonnie. "Please."

"Five dollars," Miz Marshall repeated, and drew a small ledger out of her sleeve. She wore fingerless mitts of fine lace, more suited to an evening of dancing than an afternoon at a country market. "On Señor Diaz's bay gelding."

Five dollars was a lot, but Jonnie would have it back in hand within an hour, and maybe more than that.

"Señor Diaz," I echoed as Miz Marshall stepped away again, her gown's small bustle swaying enough to catch the eye of every man down the fence. "Why, she just knows everybody, doesn't she?"

"That's her business, isn't it?"

Nobody was quite sure what Miz Marshall's business was, but it surely seemed to involve knowing people.

"Now what are you going to buy me when that five dollars comes back?" I asked, and Jonnie smiled, and the race began.

The dash ran, with Señor Diaz's bay gelding carrying it off by a hair, far as I could tell. Then there was a longer race over makeshift steeples set up in the field beyond the dirt oval, and then a cart-race for ponies. The pouch at Jonnie's belt sagged as coins filled it up, and people were always stopping off to chat to her, asking her opinion of the horses promenading in front of us. I preened a little when they looked my way, proud to sit by her side. She was known for miles around for her expertise with horseflesh, even if she was a girl and a young one at that. I'd seen her ride everything from a marsh-tackie to a stolen cavalry mount and once, on a dare, one of the cattle that ranged in the flats of the Everglades. I half-believed she could ride a Spanish boar if one came into her hands.

The Nag's Head, my parents' inn, had been so named because on its building it had been the only public house with a stable for miles around, but now folk knew it as the place to bring an animal to be trained, or to even buy a water horse that most were afraid to even try to catch.

"Lend me a ribbon, Bess," Jonnie said. She hopped down from the fence and looked at me expectantly. Her brown eyes shone, the excitement of a race to be run filling them. "For luck, fair lady."

I giggled. She always did this, acted like one of the knightly heroes from a story asking for a favor before a joust. I unwound a ribbon from my braided knot and tied it around her wrist. "How's that bite of yours?"

""Can't even feel it," she said, which didn't settle my nerves much. There were stories that limerunners' bites delivered poison like a snake, and every nasty snake I knew had a bite that numbed the flesh before turning it dead-black and rotten. It was why some folk hunted limeys, for teeth and hooves and the power they were believed to hold. "Don't worry, Bess. This one's mine."

She lifted her arm as she walked away, the red ribbon trailing from her hand like a flag.

People chattered on all sides of me, gossip and bets, and Miz Marshall came by again, but I shook my head. I never bet on Jonnie riding, even though she usually won. It seemed too much like bad luck. Instead I took a piece of lace out of my sleeve and began knitting at it. I had some idea of making a collar like Miz Marshall's, a present for Jonnie after she won, something pretty to wear at the neck of the new shirt I'd sew for her. That blood was never going to come out of what had been her best shirt and she needed a new sharp thing to wear— for church on the rare occasion that her mother got her to go… and for the night rides that had begun arriving closer and closer together this past season.

There was a part to be played on those rides, and a pretty shirt went a ways toward convincing certain people.

"Now what in God's name is that beast?" The voice came from somewhere off to my left, floating between conversation about the Methodist church's midsummer picnic and whether trout or mullet was better for smoking. "Look at them hooves. Something wrong with 'em."

It wasn't anyone I recognized straight off, nor did it sound like a man from my part of the world. The observation was followed by a hacking sound, chaw and spit hitting the dirt, and an answering voice. "Ain't never seen the like. Heard tell they're some native horse. Spanish couldn't drive 'em out."

"Evil-lookin'," the first voice said, and then subsided as I glanced left, right, seeking the voices' owners. Out on the oval, a scant handful of limerunners were reining up, their riders an assortment of the wildest men I knew—and Jonnie. Common wisdom held that to ride a limey, you had to be mad, bad, or both. The promise of the water horses savaging each other or their riders during the race had folk handing over hard-earned coin like it was sand.

Jonnie had trained every limey but one, a pitch-colored mare rode by a lanky Maroon fellow. I pondered whether that gave her an edge, or softened her up toward beasts she still had a fondness for.

The strange men's voices came to my ears again. "If the cavalry's smart about it they'll snap that boy right up. Gonna need as many good men on mounts as they can find should Abe's men come inland from Fort Leon."

The second man guffawed. "Ain't no boy. That there's a girl. I don't know as we'd be so desperate as all that." He laughed again, deep and coarse. "Hell. Conscripting girls. God forbid."

My knitting needles didn't stop, though I knew I wasn't doing my best work. The girls who worked at the inn had learned me a thing or two about eavesdropping when men talked, not to mention my ma's famous eyelash flutter and the card-player's mask on Jonnie's mother. I kept my eyes ahead and my hands busy as Jonnie's gray limerunner Keke stepped past, her split hooves stamping into the dirt. *Conscription* was a word that'd been flying through the air of late, talk of boys and men snatched from the road and off boats, pressed into service for the forces that were forming against those of the United States of America. These two, then, explained the strange military uniforms I'd seen earlier at the hog pen, gray and crisp where the Fort Leon regulars and men from the smaller river garrison wore blue.

It was already *we* and Abe's army, no bones about it. War was coming.

Blood pounded in my ears and my throat, a pulse that ticked up when the limeys burst forward on the dirt. It wasn't just the race, though every time Jonnie and Keke ran I feared some catastrophe. She glowed on the water horse's back in the settling dusk, remnants of light gilding her cheekbones and the black braid that flew out behind her. The Maroons' corpse-queen Ada Nuit at the head of her hunting band couldn't have rode prettier nor more swiftly. No matter Jonnie's boy's clothes, she was unmistakable to me—beautiful, strong—and it filled me with terror to think that the men who ran things might not care.

That she was too good with a horse to ignore.

That they might become so desperate as all that.

CHAPTER TWO

EWS TRAVELED QUICKEST ON the tongues of trappers, particularly when there were truths to be embroidered.

They clustered to the Nag's Head at all times of day, since—as Ma said—ill deeds didn't rise with the chickens: Rafael Suarez tying up at the post outside at half midnight, demanding supper though we'd already served it, and Jamie Little's ginger head popping around the door, eyes swollen from another bout of malaria but still swerving, pausing, until he spotted the girl he wanted. Susy Hen teeth, I rarely even saw her slip in, but there she'd be, hunched over checkers and swearing like half the Army's cavalry had been beating her at the game all evening.

But today they streamed in steady, starting with Jamie at first light and him not even shouting for an upstairs room. Instead he settled himself at the hearth and grinned at me. "Bess, my best love, where's that coffee?"

Well! Down to business it was, then.

The coffee was boiling when I went into the kitchen. Jonnie's mother Maria didn't turn from where she was bent over the hearth, spoon in hand, as I began arranging the coffee pot and cups. After a moment, stirring the kettle of grits, she sniffed. "They're gonna scorch anyhow. Tell that red demon his grits'll be scorched so he's not after my blood."

The grits looked all right to me, and I didn't think Jamie was so demonic, but I nodded. Maria always knew who was in the inn—or maybe she'd heard Jamie's horse as Aaron wrestled him to the stable. Jamie Little was the sort of man who'd never quite cottoned to the fact that stallions didn't make good riding mounts. Most of the trappers didn't have the patience to use limerunners for riding, only fighting and racing and selling, and some of them—like Jamie or Susy's brother Ward—made up the insult to their perceived manhood by riding the meanest warmbloods they could find. The last time Jamie had been in town, his chestnut had kicked down the stall door and gone bullet-wise after the scent of mares.

Limey mares were only interested in stallions of their own kind, but a warmblood male made for fine eating.

"At least he's on time for breakfast," I said. "Instead of riding in here looking for eggs at noon."

"Mm-hm," said Maria, never a good sign.

Grits landed in a bowl, a brownish scorched patch along the dollop's underside, and a fried egg on top of them. Fatback was extra coin unless Maria liked whomever was at table, and she didn't like most of them. The coffee smelled good, thick and gleaming-black, though I'd already had tea that morning. Some impulse made me slip a slice of bacon into the bowl and add a sugar-cellar to my tray when Maria turned to the china hutch.

She swiveled back and stacked more cups than Jamie needed into my hand. When I looked at her, she laughed. "Rose said there was mackerel sky this morning, before the sun. That's company all day, my lovely. Look bright-eyed, Bess. I'll tell you when the eggs are gone."

Ma hadn't said anything to *me* about the sky acting funny. I lifted the tray and marched it out to the inn's main room.

Ma and Maria were right about company all day, never mind what the weather said. The inn swelled to bursting, steady like the creek rising, as more trappers rode up the highway and came trudging east in damp boots from their marsh skinnies on the river, and townspeople joined them. Knots of bodies formed at tables and sprawled along benches; the eyes that flickered between faces were mistrustful, or full of questions; we were out of eggs very soon. It felt as though everyone knew something, or suspected something, scented it on the wind like hounds. The murmurs and nervy scattered laughter ground at my good temper.

I wanted in on the secret, whatever it was.

When I saw Jamie Little's arm snake out, I turned in a maneuver perfected over the years since my parents had set me in the main room and told me to be amenable to guests but not so friendly I ended up in a family way. His fingers pinched my elbow instead of what he'd been aiming for, and I smiled at him. "Jamie Little, are all these people here to see you?"

"Could be," he said, all belly and bristle, and the man with him laughed. He was younger, Solomon Rowland, accounted the handsomest of the trappers by a country mile, and even as the thought that he and Jamie weren't particular friends entered my head, I giggled at myself silently. Sol was everyone's friend, or at least I'd never seen him with a knife drawn over breakfast the way some of the other trappers got on.

"Bess," Jamie said, leaning close enough to slip his arm around my waist, "Miss Elizabeth Ramsey, would you like to hear something interesting?"

I always wanted to hear something interesting.

I disentangled myself from Jamie's pinching hand and positioned the coffee pot's spout over his cup. "More coffee? Or do the interesting things need something stronger?"

Men were good at talking, even better when a bit of oil was applied to the creaky joints of their brains. Jamie was already in a fine mood thanks to the bacon, and it was obvious he'd tied up outside with gossip burning a hole in his trouser pocket.

He slapped his stomach, chuckling, and right on cue a flask appeared in Sol's hand. He shook it swiftly over each cup and winked at me. I winked back, emptying the coffee pot, and dipped my head when Sol offered me the flask. "Solomon Rowland, you know I never indulge before noon."

I rarely indulged at all, not since Jonnie and I had stolen a jar of Miss Anthorpe the schoolmarm's aged moonshine and taken it down to the lakeshore. Jonnie had tried not to laugh at how sick I'd been. She'd smoothed my hair back and kissed me even though my face was a mess and tucked me back into bed before Ma could sniff out the telltale scent of corn liquor and vomit on her only child's best petticoat.

Sol tucked the flask into his vest pocket. He sat back in his chair, one boot crossed over the other knee, and gazed up at me with level brown eyes. "I'd take it while I can get it, Bess. We might be high and dry before too long."

"Why, how so?" I mimed horror with a hand pressed to my lips. "Has the still burned down?"

"Not hardly," Jamie said. "Those cavalry bastards—" And here he threw a glance toward the fireplace, where one such sat with space around him on each side, the Army not being popular around our parts. "They've all turned traitor, and those what haven't are deserting. Running for the coast, way I heard it." He spat onto his plate and the scraggly remnant of scorched grits. "Be dead men 'fore they reach the Atlantic."

I blinked, rubbing spots of coffee from the pot with my apron hem. "Turned traitor?"

"You ain't heard?" Jamie chuckled. He looked pleased to be the bearer of news. The Nag's Head was the hub of news, as any inn had the right to be. News came in with travelers and went out again, more sensational than it had arrived. "Why, Florida's joined the Confederacy, Bess, my sweet. The garrison at the river, it's purely overrun. Suarez was sailing past when they ran that new flag up."

"Traitor," Sol repeated. His voice sounded odd, as though he was pronouncing a foreign word never before spoken aloud. Then his face returned to its usual humor. He wagged a finger at Jamie. "Now I'd never figured you for such a patriot."

"The Union can be damned," Jamie said with a snort. "All I care is for business." He stared into the small black glimmer remaining in his cup as I'd seen some of the Maroon women do, like the coffee's surface would show him the future. "I suppose it might tick up, come to think of it. The patriotic thing to do, well, surely that's charging these Rebs twice for the same goods."

Sol chuckled appreciatively, and I smiled, smoothing a loose tendril from my forehead. The heat between kitchen and main room was beginning to work on my plaits, not to mention my mood. I longed to be away in the quiet of the room Jonnie and I shared to re-braid my hair, pick over what Jamie and Sol had said, try to tease out the true parts from the bluster as I carded hay and dirt from raw wool. I loved the whirlwind and bustle of the inn in its peak hours, and hated it at the same time: loved each new voice as it joined the ruckus, hated the point at which the words began to fall with the weight of hailstones. The customers' need to be heard pinched at my skin sharper than Jamie's fingers. I was cheerful and pretty and quick on my feet, all the best traits of an innkeeper's daughter, but sometimes even I couldn't see the change coming, the moment when my love for the inn and its strange populace soured into exhaustion and resentment.

"Where's that girl of yours?" Sol said as I began gathering his plate and Jamie's onto my tray. "I've got a buyer looking for a feral limey."

"I'll tell her you asked."

Sol stood and took the tray from my hands. He was quite tall when standing and even if I'd had a mind not to relinquish the tray I couldn't have stopped him. He smiled down at me. "Maybe I'll give you the details to pass along."

Jamie laughed again, a boisterous snort, and this time his hand landed where he aimed it: squarely over the rump of my dress. I laughed too, a yelp so loud my mother turned from the bar with eagle eyes. She peered through the horde of patrons at the three of us, then called across the room.

"Quit idling and get that to the kitchen, Elizabeth."

I wasn't idling and all of us knew it, but sometimes pretenses had to be maintained.

My mother's mother had chosen the land for the Nag's Head because of its height: the highest rise in a low country of marshland, broad rivers, and the shimmering, vast Lake of Spirits to the southwest. It was a local legend, Sarah Cunningham and the pension given to her after her husband was lost at sea; Ma treasured the story, kept it close like the locket worn around her throat. It was said that my grandmother had built the narrow walk on the inn's roof to watch for her husband, though even on the fairest of days a body couldn't see all the way east to the Atlantic Ocean.

I'd never been to the Atlantic myself, but Okeechobee seemed just as magnificent.

It gleamed as dusk fell outside my window, its surface placid. A white pinprick far west, barely visible at the water's rim, was a boat—fishermen, based on the low sail.

The river trappers and other smugglers who worked the waters preferred barges, canoes, and small fast cutters, depending on their cargo.

They also took more care not to broadcast their presence to onlookers.

The scent of the marshes reached my nose as I sewed, my window open for the breeze in the heady summer twilight, and I breathed deep. My needle's motion became swifter, automatic, crimson thread a shade darker than the jacket's fabric whipping along cuffs and lapel. A sound reached my ears, distantly, a twinkle of music that—half-dazed, caught in the web that embroidery spun around my mind—I thought came from outside. A few of the upstairs girls carousing in the lane with lovers, perhaps, or the priest at the little Spanish Catholic church chanting vespers.

"That's pretty," Jonnie said, and closed the bedroom door behind herself.

My fingers kept the needle moving as my mind came back to itself, my throat closing around the snip of song. After a moment I said, "I'll be done soon. Not a moment and you'll be ready to leave. Only—"

"Only?" She smiled, moving to stand behind my chair. A hand caressed the crown of my head, and then her fingers curled in my hair, unraveling the remnants of braids. "Bess, what is it?"

Only be safe, I wanted to cry to her, as I always did, but there was no fortune in that.

"You don't need these, do you?" she asked, lifting the thickest plait. I shook my head. "Then let me comb it for you."

Embroidery sprouted under my fingers while hers drew a bone comb through my hair, gently smoothing away tangles and bits of hay gathered from fetching a keg of ale from the barn when Pa had been too busy earlier. The designs laid into the jacket's lapels said one thing, its hems another; there were curlicues and narrow petals, spindly leaves and long-legged birds masking the symbols Jonnie would carry with her to the coast. The red velvet was well-made, too thick for summer warmth, but in the chill of deepest night she liked the close feeling, the heaviness. She said she could feel the stitches protecting her, swore the velvet would deflect a bullet, which wasn't anything I wanted to test. She'd kiss me in a moment, a braid between her fingers, and marvel at the skill of my hands, as she did when she stood in the river and roped a limerunner with a lasso I'd knotted for her.

She shook it aside when I reminded her that Rafael Suarez had taught me sailor's knots, and Miss Anthorpe my finest embroidery stitches, and Jonnie's own mother the clever little ways of tying thread and twine and even hair to secure power. It might've been others' knowledge, Jonnie said, but it was my hands—both of them lifted, her lips pressed to the palms in turn—that turned craft into solid reality.

I snipped off the last thread between my teeth and knotted it, then kissed the fabric and smoothed the lapel back down. "There. Yet again."

"There," Jonnie said, her voice very close to my ear. I wanted to lean sideways and peek at the mirror to see what she'd done to my hair, but I wanted all the more to stay as I was, circled in her arms with her breath on my skin. We'd grown up in this room, the inn's garret, tucked above the rooms where women and a few men sometimes plied a trade Pa hadn't been too eager to have in the house.

Ungodly, he'd grumbled when Jonnie and I were stashed beneath the windowsill outside listening to him and Ma have it out, but Ma had prevailed. To her way of thinking men would seek what they would, and best if there was some control over it—some guarantee of safety, and the Nag's Head was respected as all inns were, neutral and belonging to all people who used them. If the rites of hospitality cloaked trappers' gambling and piracy, according to Ma, they would cover also certain nighttime activities, whatever Pa or the Catholic priest or the Methodist ladies thought about it.

At any rate, neither Sunday school nor the goings-on below our floorboards had affected the shape of my relationship with Jonnie. Hers was the first face I could remember seeing, even before my parents' or Maria's, and I had never not loved it, and what was between us would never die, only change form a little as it grew with the years. That was right. That was godly.

After a while she shifted, her arms dropping as she crouched in front of me. One hand stroked the velvet jacket where it lay across my knees. "How many more, do you think?"

She didn't mean how many more messages would she have to carry to the Union men at the coast, but how many more messages the jacket itself could bear. Velvet would only take so many stitches before it became worn, too thin to hold the embroidery—and the stitches I set worked that much faster, because they were more than their curves and edges. They held truth in them, and power, words the men could read and words no one but I could speak, aloud or in thread.

It tore at me every time, Jonnie riding out like a living flame beneath the moon, and I only able to protect her a little.

"Twice more," I said. "Three, maybe. Don't worry. It's sturdy." I lifted the jacket and we admired it together, its wide lapels and high collar, its tails flaring from a narrow waist and gold-filigree buttons down its front. Jonnie saved money from her wages and sales for the materials, and I'd designed it and put it together, and the jacket was the best of both of us holding her tight. "You best get it on. I hear Keke tromping around down there, all antsy."

Jonnie giggled. "She can wait a touch longer." She stood, pulling me with her and close against her, and one hand came up to cup my cheek. "Bess."

"Johanna." Her full name for her father John, lost to slave-catchers in Georgia. "Miss Jonnie Bruner, terror of the road."

"It was Sol?" She stepped back from me and took the jacket from my hands, turning to the bureau. "How'd you get him away from Jamie? Lord God, that man's mouth. What do you bet he ends up dead before summer's done? Talking so big about the Rebs in the garrison and all."

I didn't like to think of Jamie Little dead, by anyone's hand. He wasn't exactly a good man—none of the trappers could be termed such—but he was part of my life, like alligators and tales of Ada Nuit, spotted hounds and the miry mud between river and marsh.

"I didn't," I said, watching her remove the patched shirt she'd been wearing all day and shake out her new muslin blouse. "He made his reasons to go into the kitchen."

"Sure he did." In the mirror, Jonnie's face grimaced. She buttoned the blouse with sharp movements. "Grinned at you and winked those pretty eyes and let everyone think exactly what they—"

Her grumbling became a shriek when I grabbed her around the waist. The strong muscles of her stomach rippled beneath my palm, and she let me turn her until it was my fingers on the blouse's buttons. Her face smoothed from its frown into the expression I loved most, her broad cheekbones serene and her deep brown eyes heavy, lips softly parted. She allowed me to lift her arms and slide them into the jacket sleeves, doll-like, and then she gave a twirl. The blouse's lace collar bobbed beneath her chin.

My heart ached to see her: girlish, suddenly just seventeen, my age. She liked people to think she was older, though the whole town knew her age, that Maria had fled down Florida's length with Jonnie growing inside her. She liked to be thought tough, capable, dangerous as any of the trappers, and those things were true. But the ticklish softness at the hollow of her throat was true, too, and the scars on her arms from feral limeys' teeth, and her face when she was praying at night before we slept.

"What do they say?" she asked, examining the coat's lapels. She always asked, and I never told her, though it would have been meaningless to both of us. That was the deal, how the Northerners wanted it. They thought it a fine trick, the red jacket, so bold no one would think the person wearing it wanted anything but to be seen—seen by anyone and everyone, and people who wanted to be seen weren't people with things to hide.

It was always hard to resist telling Jonnie the coded words, but never more difficult than right now.

"The Confederate forces," I whispered, my throat tight. Perhaps she'd be satisfied with just a peek. "They're at the garrison now, you know."

"I know." Her voice was impatient, her hands busily buttoning the coat and drawing her boots on over breeches. "That can't be the message. Everyone knows the garrison is theirs. And that they got their eye on the navy at Fort Leon."

That was too much. She was too smart, she'd catch it.

She finished buckling her belt across her hips and turned to me. My breath caught as it always did to see her dressed so, the flexible leather of her boots fitted to her thighs and shining-black in the lamplight. Color climbed into her cheeks, a rosy flush that reflected the jacket and only heightened her beauty, that vivid heat and her chin's stubborn tilt and the steely flash of her eyes. She didn't need the twin pistols at her belt, nor the cutlass Rafael Suarez and Joseph Fletcher had taught her to use, not with a gaze like that. But I was glad she had them.

Outside the window, a hoarse whicker sounded. Jonnie laughed back.

"So what are the Rebs after, then?"

I put my hand to my head, stroking the simple braids she'd left in my hair. "Keep Keke safe. Let her keep you safe."

Jonnie stared at me, and finally gave a slow nod. "Of course."

She diverted my hand from its worrying and kissed it, then went to the window. The two-story jump to the porch roof was nothing for Jonnie's strong legs, and the short drop after that negligible when a sturdy mount waited below, but though Keke was well-trained, I wouldn't have called her *sturdy*. Not for nothing had Jonnie named her a short version of a word from Maria's country, a name that meant tiny, a scrap, little bit. Nonetheless Keke caught Jonnie when she dropped, and I made myself watch them trot out of the yard. The crimson jacket stayed in my eyes until they burned, yearning to blink or cry.

There was only one thing the Confederacy could want in our part of Florida—the part where little grew but scrub pines and stubby palms and generations of cowmen had lost cattle to the muck and mosquitoes. There was no northward path for the Confederacy out of Florida but through control of the rivers and coastal waterways. There was no resource to be bought up that could provide them that control save the strangest on Florida soil, and the most devastating for a military force.

Limerunners.

CHAPTER THREE

OR JONNIE'S SIXTH BIRTHDAY we'd gone swimming in the Sanctus River. My pa manned the inn while Ma and Maria traipsed through the scrub with baskets in hand because Jonnie had begged to have a picnic. There was dense, sweet cornbread hiding beneath those kerchiefs, and fried frog legs and cold boiled shrimp and molasses cookies and I was more interested in sitting under a low-spreading oak and getting down to lunch than running into the Sanctus.

Jonnie was a good swimmer. Maria made sure of that. The man who'd enslaved her in South Carolina whipped any of his plantation workers who went near water, and Maria had only learned to swim by necessity on her journey south. It was hard to pass through Florida without finding yourself in a body of water at least once, and upon her arrival in Sawgrass, she'd surveyed the boys who dunked themselves in the rivers and Lake Okeechobee without a care and determined to follow suit.

The Maroon women on the lake's fringes taught her to paddle a canoe and swim underwater for near three minutes without coming up, and most importantly how to tell limey tracks in the sandy banks from those of deer. It was one thing to swim in open water, where you could see one of the beasts coming, and another entirely to happen on its tracks first and not mark them—go flinging yourself into a creek in dense, dark growth where the water horses' sleek bodies tangled among the mangrove roots and you might not come back up.

The Maroons and white settlers alike told Maria exactly what to expect if you met a limey on its own turf, but Maria already knew.

Sometimes in those days, abed at night, we'd plead for a story and Maria would ask what kind, and Jonnie always wanted the story of the limerunner at Fort Gates.

Don't you be so bloody-minded, my girl. Now how 'bout a story with a princess and a tower?

That day the sun had been so hot even my attention turned from the picnic to the water soon enough. I took a cookie in each hand down to where Jonnie crouched in the shallows with her skirt kilted up and gave her one. She ate it absently, eyes trained on the water trickling slowly over her brown toes. It was cold, so cold I squealed, for the Sanctus bubbled up out of a spring. It was clear and fresh, not the murky half-salt of the big St. Johns running into Okeechobee. It was held holy—you could tell from the name, Pa said, left behind by the Spanish looking for gold and eternal life—but some said instead it was the mouth of Hell. Caverns lurked below the surface, and sometimes bones swept south when the river ran high after a rainfall, the bones of folk who'd drowned in the blue depths.

It was said limerunners were born from cold springs like that, though they lived more often along the marshes and narrow creeks that flowed like hair from the St. Johns River.

Jonnie showed me what she was looking at so hard. Her cheeks still full of molasses cookie, she scooped her fingers into the water and brought up a handful of teeth. There were some the size of my thumb, triangular and near-black, and some much larger and whitish, curved wicked-sharp against Jonnie's palm. Those were so long that I wondered if they were pieces of antler, broken when bucks fought in the autumn. I grabbed one with my silly small girl's hands that had to clutch everything that caught my eye, and immediately blood welled from my palm. Bright drops appeared on the tips of my pointer, middle and marriage fingers, strung out like a jeweled necklace. I dropped the tooth and shoved my fingers into my mouth, and Jonnie watched, quiet, as a red blot wavered in the water and dissolved.

Hands descended onto both of our shoulders then, dragging us back up the bank on our bottoms. It was Ma, her lips white around the edges. I waited for her to scold me—just me, never Jonnie—but instead she gathered the two of us up, one under each arm. She had burly arms; sometimes she held the horses while Pa shoed them, and sometimes she hefted kegs of beer from the hayloft, and two six-year-old girls were nothing to restrain. It was Maria further up the bank who scared me right then, my attention diverted from the sting in my fingers. Jonnie's mother sat with her legs tucked beneath her skirt and her eyes straight ahead, glaring past us and onto the river. Her hands were busily braiding a piece of sawgrass she'd separated into skinny strands, and despite the grass's sharp edges her fingers were whole. They seemed to know exactly what they were doing, working independent of her eyes.

As Ma stopped next to Maria and pushed Jonnie and me behind her legs, I peeked back to see what Maria was staring at. It wasn't an alligator in the river, nor a water moccasin swimming faster than we could, nor even a trapper ready to rob the remnants of our picnic, but a gleaming brown horse. It was smaller than our draft horse Buck, and smaller than our cart horse Spots, dainty as a doe deer and the strangest animal I'd seen. Its ears pricked, longer than a normal horse's and black-peaked. It stared right back at us with eyes that pointed forward instead of being placed on the sides of its head like those of Buck and Spots.

Maria's hands worked faster, the sawgrass strips turning into a fancy braid.

The water horse dipped its snout to the river and snuffled. Then it stepped away, its stilt legs cleaving down clean, barely leaving a ripple behind. Its naked tail whipped once, twice, and then it was gone… or maybe it was just that I couldn't see it anymore, that it had become the same as the shadow-striped water and the bushes and trees tangled along its banks.

A little later Maria threw the sawgrass braid into the small fire Ma had built, and we went home.

On the way I asked Maria about the sawgrass, what she'd been doing, and she said that a braid or a knot kept things together, the way the weave of cloth made wool keep its shape as a shirt. She said if you wanted it enough, and knew how, you could braid love into a person's heart or unravel a plait to pull it out of someone else's.

I looked at my hand in Jonnie's and decided that the way our fingers fit together was sort of a braid, and maybe that was what Maria meant. I thought about Ma combing my hair at night and pulling the strands into a plait and kissing me. I thought about how Jonnie had watched the water horse with a look on her face like she was gazing at the painting of Jesus in my parents' big Bible.

She hadn't been afraid at all.

After that, all the tales that got told in our part of Florida about limeys felt real, like the creatures were waiting just around a bend in the trail. Jonnie had always loved horses, but she began begging Pa to let her ride Spots around the meadow behind the inn, let her clutch on behind him when he rode Spots to town, let her practice putting the saddle on Spots' patient old back, though she was so small she barely came up to the gelding's black-and-white chest. She'd taken one of the long, sharp teeth that we now knew were limey teeth from the river and kept it in a box with our other treasures. She hoarded stories of limeys from the trappers who passed through and went hunting with my father, learned to hold herself still and downwind of prey—and maybe it was to shoot deer or bear, as Pa said, but I could see her yearning to try to catch a limey with all she'd learned.

They were the shape of Florida itself, long and jagged-edged, deadly. Folk traveling through said limeys lived north of us too, scattered through the inland wherever springs bubbled and saltwater met fresh, but the shores of the Lake of Spirits were their homeland. They were thicker in the brush here than elsewhere, and Jonnie was boastful of that. She'd point to the sign swinging above the inn's door, the black horse's head embellished with a red eye and sharp teeth. She'd tell newcomers of the races held and how a limey was as like to kill its rider as win her laurels. She'd caution them not to go hunting on dark moons, when

Ada Nuit ranged abroad with her troop of corpse-ridden water horses. She'd speak of the ways to catch a limey for breaking or butchering: how a brave soul could stand in the shallows with a lasso, and one braver still could prick their finger and let blood drop into the water and wait, so still, until the limey came to her.

After a while, Maria gave up trying to stem Jonnie's love, and began teaching me her ways with knots and thread instead.

Swathed in his beekeeping kit, Pa looked more for-midable than any of the men at the river garrison. He'd frightened me as a child, the first time I saw him out-fitted as such: long full sleeves covering the dark hair of his arms, a broad-brimmed hat draped in net blurring his face, a glowing smudge in one hand with which to smoke the bees. Somehow it had been worse when he took off his hat inside the kitchen and offered me a slab of honeycomb and became my father again.

He touched his hat-brim as we passed one another in the inn's yard, and I knew he was frowning behind the netting. Several years before, grudgingly, he'd decided that if I was going to feed the limerunners while we had them penned, I'd need a kit similar to his in case they went wild and tried to get at me. Jonnie'd laughed as we all discussed it over dinner, and then harder when I came tottering out the kitchen door in several layers of wool and leather gloves Ma had cobbled together with pieces from the blacksmith.

Jonnie had known it wouldn't work.

"Get there," I said to the bay limey where he stood, glaring at me from twenty paces. They didn't like meat already killed, but Ma didn't like to hear chickens squawking as they were devoured outside her windows. Said it put the guests off their own feed. "Well, or don't. See if I care."

If we'd been able to keep them in the barn with the other horses, nobody would've been within earshot of their dinner. But limeys were funny creatures in all ways, and they didn't take to hay and sawdust for their beds, nor a covered roof above them. The pen Jonnie and Pa had built was trenched down to a limestone slab, into which the water horses were always digging their hooves, and constructed of oak rather than pine. It held ditches of brackish water same as the barn at the Sawyer racing oval, and its roof was open to the sky. I'd seen the beasts wriggling during rainstorms, as coltish and near to being cute as they ever got.

The gray snapped her jaws when I tossed a hen into her stall. She was a lighter gray than Jonnie's Keke, the color of clouds, and closer to being trained than the bay boy. A limey was never broken, not really, not until you killed it; they were tame, sometimes, after long years of effort, and even then most folk didn't trust them not to turn on a knife-blade. But you sure could train them, the way a warmblood horse or a dog took to training. Some people paid more money for them half-wild, like the ones we'd taken to market. These two Pa had a buyer for, a man with exact specifications.

The scent of blood rose as they finally tore into their dinner.

I perched on the fencepost, well enough away, and began unpinning my braids. Whenever I went into the pen my hair was up, tight and controlled, no loose strands or long enticing curls to catch the limeys' eyes. They were biters, and alert to any unexpected movement. Their instinct was to take such movement as a threat and go for it. Nearly tame ones, like these two, were used to how I smelled, but that didn't mean they'd never try to get at me through the pen's slats. It was like the ill-fated protective clothing Pa had tried. You couldn't fool a limey with wool the way you could a beehive with smoke, and they didn't like gloved hands.

A year or so back we'd been up to the races at Sawyer and Jonnie had tried to tell a boy that his mount wouldn't take to it, him managing it with gloves. It hadn't been the first time I'd seen a limerunner tear into human flesh, but it'd been messy nonetheless.

I sighed and ran my hands through my hair. Six braids loosened around my fingers, and the large knot into which they'd all been woven dropped open. The heavy weight of it shifted, tension flowing out of my shoulders. It was another of Maria's little nothings; she called them that because they didn't work if you thought about them head-on as you would a sum or a Bible verse. Each of the six braids was something I wanted to keep safe and well, and together they made up the whole of me. It was all the protection I had between me and jaws that could drag down a gator, but it wasn't a style suitable for serving guests inside.

Something tugged a strand of my hair. "I'd surely love to help you with that, Miss Bess."

I smiled, keeping sweet while moving my head away from Warren Almquist's hand. "Don't you know better than to disturb a lady's toilette? Why, I heard a gal up in Ocoee shot her sweetheart because he startled her getting dressed. Popped right up in her mirror like a ghoul and she just turned around and shot him."

Seemed like a fine excuse for killing a man, if you asked me.

Warren scoffed, grinning at me. "You gonna shoot me today, Bess?"

"I might, you don't stop finicking around with these beasts." My hands worked quickly, shaping a braid that began along my hairline and curved around my head to trail off loose into curls, bound with a ribbon fished from my bodice. Guests liked a pretty countenance bringing them venison and coffee. "Don't I usually find you in the stable eyeing other men's horses? You developing a taste for limeys now too?"

He followed me when I slid down from the fence and made for the inn. "Heard tell a limey killed a man last night on the Leon road. What do you think about that?"

"I think that doesn't sound like news," I said, and let him hold the inn's doors for me.

"Weren't no wild one neither," Warren continued. He was close behind me as the noise of the main room closed over us, practically stomping on my hem with his sandy boots. "Three wagons was set on and all the cargo taken, a whole passel of slaves run cowering to the Maroon camp. If you think the trappers aren't hot about that—"

I stopped at the longest table and turned, beaming up at Warren. "Now why don't you set right down here and I'll bring you something cool to drink?"

It was hateful, being sweet to him, but inside the Nag's Head he wasn't just silly old Warren Almquist, whom Jonnie and I had grown up with, gone to Sunday school with, run from after school when he and the other boys tried to tug up our skirts. A guest was a guest, even if they were ugly and whitish-haired and didn't know a horse's hoof from his hind end and spread nasty gossip to boot.

A limey killing a man was one thing. The wild ones couldn't be reckoned with, especially if they snuck up on you, and most of the people interested in training them only taught them to fight. It could've been anyone tussling with trappers and leaving a body behind. But Jonnie had been on the highway to Fort Leon last night. Her Keke was well capable of killing a man and leaving others alive to tell the tale. She'd have been all fired up yesterday evening after she left Sawgrass, burning with the message I'd sewn into her coat and let slip because I was weak for her, itching to the bone with righteous rage over her water horses. If an opportunity dropped into her path—

Maria had taught us to hate the sight of folk being kicked to the coast for sale, or dragged back north in chains.

I went through the kitchen doors, turning my face to hide a smile in my hair. Maybe it was bad of her and we'd hear about it soon enough, but that was the law of the land. It was like she'd told me: you were rich enough to buy a good horse, or smart enough to steal one. You were strong enough, wily enough, to keep hold of what was yours, or it became someone else's. No trapper would argue against their own code, even when it was them on the losing end of it.

Somebody needed to warn the Confederate men just who limerunners belonged to, but it sure wasn't going to be me.

CHAPTER FOUR

*S*HE WAS IN THE kitchen when I came in, sitting at the table in her undershirt as Maria sewed up a gash in her arm. The bite over her ribs had begun to seep again too; blood showed through her shirt. The sight of her in pain, hurt again and so soon, drove any humor I'd thought to find in the situation right out of my head.

"What happened?" I dropped my armload of dishes into the sink, so carelessly Ma turned from the stove to scold. "Jonnie, Warren Almquist said—"

"Oh, Warren," Jonnie said, sarcastic, though I heard the grit in her teeth. "Well, seeing as we all know truth flows from his mouth like honey..."

Maria brought her own mouth close to Jonnie's arm and snipped the thread between her teeth. "Hold still, my girl."

"He said," I repeated, raising my voice so Ma could hear me over the pots boiling on the stove, "that you killed a man on the Leon highway last night. Hmm? Your Union men command you to do that?"

"He told you that?" she said right back. "Lying sack of—"

"Johanna," Maria said.

At the stove, Ma stirred furiously, her face red with heat and anger. Her mouth pulled tight as she glanced between Jonnie and me. Sometimes Maria was hard to read, but Ma was an open book: she laughed when we made jokes, cried when one of us turned up with a scraped knee, and right now she was furious. I just wasn't sure which direction her fury was aimed.

"He said a limey killed a trapper after its rider attacked slave wagons," I said.

Jonnie shrugged, all casual, and the worry I'd felt burned right away, ash beneath the flame of rage in my chest. The red velvet jacket was tossed across the back of her chair, a rip showing in the left sleeve. I went to the table and touched it instead of her. The problem was I was too like Ma, sometimes. I didn't know what I was angry at just now, either.

"Three wagons. How'd you think you'd come away alive?"

"Well, I did, didn't I?" She didn't look at me but at the coat in my hands, and I watched a sliver of shame tug her lips. "Bess. Don't worry."

"How'm I not to worry?" I lifted the jacket to give my fingers something to do, because they were itching and so were my eyes. "Maria, tell her. Ma—"

Ma shook her head, her long brown braid arrow-straight down her back.

"A slavers' caravan, Bess," was all Maria said.

"They said," I started, hating the quaver in my voice. "When all this started they said—those men said all you'd do was ride them messages back and forth! No one said anything about raiding trappers! Who was it, Jonnie? They knew you?"

There were trappers in our main room right now, supping and drinking and dicing just as always. I'd gone among three or four I knew and another two I didn't, and as the day grew on more would appear, just as always. There were enough of them between here and Okeechobee and the coast to burn the Nag's Head down around our ears if the notion took them. It wouldn't matter that the Ramsey inn had always been a no-man's-land safe for trappers and smugglers, soldiers and prostitutes and priests alike, not if enough of them decided their livelihood had been threatened by a no-account little girl.

Who was it Keke had left bleeding in the highway? Rafael Suarez? Ward Henteeth? Gil Kenyon, who'd terrified me from the time I could walk with his knotted black beard and pale eyes and his voice that'd never come back right from a throat-slitting?

"One Davey Stone," someone said from the kitchen door. Sol Rowland lounged there, hands tucked into his pockets. He smiled at the expression on Jonnie's face. "Unless the gossip misses its mark."

It wasn't a name I knew. Jonnie shrugged again. "Some white boy, barely had a beard. The other two scarpered."

"The slaves made it to Haasi Town, as I heard it." Sol studied the jacket still in my hands. "A good thing you didn't bring Miss Bess's handiwork to harm until after its message was delivered, eh, Miss Jonnie?"

A flush spread over her cheeks. "I'm sorry, Bess. Can you fix it?"

I already had plans for fixing my poor beautiful jacket's sleeve. "Maria, please? Please tell her—"

"Tell her what?" Maria said, staring straight at me. Ma brought a damp lump of leaves from the stove and placed the poultice on Jonnie's arm. "Tell her not to do what's proper?"

Tell her you love her too much for this, I wanted to yell, but Maria did love her daughter. It was just a different kind of love from mine. Maria's love frightened me sometimes, with its depth. I'd never met anyone who felt the way she did, fathomless like the Lake of Spirits. Her tales of her lost husband were filled with such fervent love I half-believed she'd conjure the man right up just by speaking of him. The other side of that love's coin was hatred for slave-owners and those men who rode through now and then, snatching up any black person in sight, never mind if they'd been born free.

Maria would never tell her daughter to set her own safety above that of people in bondage.

"It don't matter, Bess," Jonnie said. She slipped her hand into mine, cautious, like I'd push her away. "The Union men got the message about—" She glanced at Ma, then at Sol. "They said keep an eye open when I rode back, but it was to watch for Rebs running about taking boys and men for their military, not slave-catchers."

Conscription, just like the Rebs at the market-day races had said. If this plan of theirs with the limeys went on, they'd look aside from the color of Jonnie's skin, and her sex. They'd force her to catch the water horses and break them, train them to be even fiercer than they were born. And soon they'd have a whole stash of mounts as good as living weapons, the terror of the waterways, and the Union wouldn't know what hit them.

"And why not?" she continued. Her eyes narrowed and her fingers tightened around mine. "I know these roads better than them. I can go farther in a night than a trapper can with a horse or a boat—no offense, Sol." Sol lifted a hand palm-up as though to say, *who's wrong?* "I sure can't see a reason to let anybody, Reb or trapper or anybody, steal people." She took a breath and gazed up at me, her broad-open face filled with hurt. "Steal horses."

It had been a mistake, letting her figure out the message she'd carried last night.

"I mean to harry them 'til they bleed," Jonnie said, and I knew it for truth.

There was nothing more to be said, then. I felt her words sink through me like stones thrown into water. She was immovable sometimes, no matter what I tried and no matter how well I knew her, knew how to bend and coax and reason. And now her hand moved in mine, rein-rough palm pressed close, and a fiery urgency bloomed in her dark eyes. "Bess…"

Forgive me, I mouthed silently, imagining her contrite. *Believe in me,* as though I'd ever do else. But what she said next was swift and murmured, her head turned so that the loose weight of her braid masked her mouth and cheek, her voice muffled into my skin as she brought our hands to her lips in a kiss.

"Bess, I saw something."

Before I could react, Maria stood up abruptly. "Come with me, Jonnie girl. I'll wager on that cut going rancid if it don't see my heal-all and soon."

She bustled past Sol Rowland, so fast and hard-stepping she knocked him loose from the doorframe, and her skirt disappeared down the hallway. Jonnie blinked after her, looking near-foolish. Ma hadn't spoken a word the whole time I'd been in the kitchen. She came back to the table and removed the camphor leaves from Jonnie's arm, then looked at me. "Bess, see to those potatoes. Almquist called for dinner near an hour past, now. Don't you think you'd better be getting to work?"

I didn't want to get to work. I wanted to carry Jonnie upstairs and go over every inch of her with the magnifying glass Pa kept on the mantel in his and Ma's bedroom for reading the Bible on Sunday evenings because, no matter what he said, his eyes were starting to fade. I wanted to look at the stitch Maria had used on Jonnie's arm, and wash the bite in her side again, and kiss her until nothing hurt anymore. I wanted to know what she'd seen, if it was so strange and wondrous as all that, so bad that she hadn't wanted our mothers or Sol to hear her whisper it to me. I wanted to lock her in the garret to keep her from getting to Keke, or beg her to catch a boat to Hispaniola the next time Rafael Suarez got all gallant and offered to spirit me away, or ride Spots to the garrison and burn it down myself, but I did not want to get to work. But then there was little in our part of the land that wasn't work. It was cruel country; everyone worked, and Maria and Jonnie, they thought their work came from God Himself.

A little while after I'd served the elder and younger Almquists their sweet potatoes and squirrel pie, Warren tried to stick his boar knife into Sol Rowland.

He didn't succeed, though Sol went down onto the carpet like a calving heifer and Warren piled on top of him, stabbing at anything that moved with one hand and knocking his fist into Sol's face with the other.

"Sol!" I yelped before I could help myself. It wasn't as though fights were uncommon, the amount of rough men we had in and out of the inn, but everyone liked Sol. He wasn't usually on the receiving end of hard feelings, and any number of ladies would be sad to see his handsome face damaged, including the one who'd been sitting on his lap. "Warren, you let him be 'fore I call my father."

"Cheating son of a whore," Warren snarled, an odd choice of insult to my way of thinking, considering more than a few whores were known to frequent Warren's company. You'd have thought his feelings toward them would be warmer. "Twice now I seen you—"

"Christ mercy, boy," Sol said. He shoved Warren off and stood, rubbing the back of a hand across his jaw. Blood trickled into his beard. "I wouldn't like to see your nerves with something more than a few bits on the line."

I doubted Sol had cheated at cards. Warren just wasn't very good at losing. Come to think of it, he wasn't much good at anything.

"A few bits?" I chanced a look at the cards table while Warren fumed. Indeed, the heap of coin at Sol's place far outweighed the few scattered at Warren's. Then I shrank back as Warren snarled, "By God, I'll take it out of your hide."

A pistol was snuggled up to Warren's bobbing Adam's apple before I could blink. "Try it, whelp."

"Sol," I said again, quieter.

For a moment the whole room seemed to quiver: the other men at their dice, Warren's father the miller and Jamie Little conferring over a shipment of cedar wood, the upstairs girls now clustered along the wall and twittering at one another, my father behind the bar and Aaron the horse-boy poised in the kitchen door with a stack of firewood. The men's rifles and shotguns were hung at the front doors, as was the rule of the house, but every hand strained toward a knife or pistol. Then Sol looked down at me and smiled.

"You've gone and scared Miss Bess." He released Warren with a shove, sending him backward into his chair, and returned his pistol to its holster, slung between shoulder and armpit. "Perhaps you'll win it back in a minute here."

I sensed Warren wouldn't be winning anything at all today.

Irritation boiling beneath my ribs, I began clearing coffee cups and tin mugs and plates with rounds of pone still on them, never mind if the men had intended to eat them. Those would be tossed to the hogs—or maybe I'd crumble them up for the chickens. None of the men in the main room, I decided, deserved even a bit of sweet corn pone, and that included Sol. He was stronger and smarter than Warren Almquist, older, more experienced—more a man in every way that folk counted, as far as I'd heard from the ruckus that kicked up beneath the garret's floorboards when he went visiting Anne Sloakum—it was like a hawk toying with a bantam. Not a fair fight in the slightest. Beneath him.

"That boy," Almquist the miller grumbled as I brushed by to collect his plate. "Old enough to pay his debts, or I'll know why."

I wondered just how much money Warren had lost at cards today.

Almquist and Jamie Little's conversation trailed away into the price of horseflesh and how they might go about bilking the Rebel military. Pa waved me behind the bar after I returned from the kitchen, empty of servingware.

"You mind yourself and the room for a moment, missy. Three tired horses in the yard and Aaron needs a hand. Seeing as our Jonnie's indisposed." He kissed the top of my head quickly. "Holler if they get to squalling again."

Any of them got to squalling again, I'd whistle Jonnie's limey up from the stable and turn her loose among the benches.

I settled my nerves by rubbing down the bar nice and slow. The red wood gleamed as I dragged a damp cloth over it methodically, digging my thumbnail into each whorl and crack. It was a legend same as the rest of the stories that whirled around my mother's mother, a solid oak slab brought over from the west of England on a boat, bequeathed to the bride and her new sailor husband as a wedding gift. It had weathered hurricanes, a fire, the loss of my grandfather to the waves, and much vomit courtesy of drunken trappers, its sheen remaining undiminished. Once, when we'd been about twelve years old, Jonnie had laid her head on the counter to watch me dust, run her fingers over the wood and told me all dreamy-like that it was the color of a limey she'd seen in the creek that morning. *Blood bay, Bess.*

Limeys were all blood, so I'd figured, cold-blooded like eels and snakes, and they drank blood like mosquitoes, or that was how the stories went. I didn't know 'til later that it just meant a brown coat with red in it. Jonnie got all poetic over horses and limeys like some girls did over boys.

What had her dreamy eyes seen last night, among the blood and gunfire? Whatever it was, it would have to wait at least until Pa returned from horse-wrangling.

Never mind the men's bad behavior, I did like having the big room to myself. I got to set things in order the way I pleased. The small array of glasses for slugs of liquor got polished and arranged just so across the back of the bar, and the tin cups for beer, milk, and water I hung from hooks above. I took off the apron onto which someone had slopped gravy and tied on a clean one, knotting the strings in front of my belly in a double bow. *A bow to close and another to keep, drum-tight and safe as sleep.* That was one I'd made up, a new entry into Maria's little nothings, and Maria had been impressed. Me, I wanted the eyes of the inn's guests on me exactly enough to make them mind me, leave me tips, behave themselves and believe just a bit that I might go walking with them—and that was quite enough. No hands beneath my skirts, no man's business anywhere near mine. The apron was like a knight's armor, as much as my ribbons became Jonnie's favor and her embroidered jacket cupped her safe and close.

"That was a little impressive, Miss Bess." The voice came sliding out of the room's hubbub like a rattler's tail in the sawgrass. "Why, Solomon Rowland minds you more than he ever did his mother, I'm sure."

Miz Marshall stood in front of the bar, hands folded in her fancy lace gloves and smiling at me. It wasn't too often we saw her in Sawgrass, and a little thrill went through my stomach. "Miz Marshall. I get you anything to drink? It's a warm day out there."

"Just some cold water," she said. "I don't indulge when I'm on business."

Still and all, she sipped at her tin cup like it contained the fanciest French wine. I kept an eye on the room and one on her, pondering her business. I suspected it had something to do with the girls, who'd by now gone back to their affairs of petting men's heads and kissing their dice and laughing at their jokes, no matter if they found them funny. One or two of them eyed Miz Marshall like they had something to say to her.

"I say, Miss Bess." Her eyes were bright blue. She was complected just like one of the women in Godey's, water-color-tinted and rosy. "These hangings, they're yours, is that right?"

She meant the curtains on the bar's cabinets, short and frilly-white, and those at the front windows, and the embroideries framed on the walls. I nodded. "Yes, ma'am."

"And those pretty ribbons," she went on, inclining her head toward the bosom of my dress, where I'd woven a narrow blue ribbon through the neckline. "My, it's something to behold, a country girl like you making beauty out of nothing in these parts. I doubt Ada Nuit herself could weave the clouds any more finely! And of course your lovely hair. Such braids I never did see."

I'd done my braids hastily today, seeing as Warren had been bothering me with the limeys, but I blushed nonetheless. "Thank you, ma'am."

"I wonder if I might obtain your services," Miz Marshall said. She set her cup aside and let her head tip again, this time toward Anne Sloakum and a girl named Irene who sat on a lounge near the hearth. "In due time I'll have need of a gal with clever fingers, to make these ladies look as lovely as possible."

I thought Anne and Irene and the rest were lovely enough, and the people who passed through the inn seemed to agree. I also hadn't known Miz Marshall had any say in how they looked. If there was a madam about it was Ma, but mainly the women saw to themselves.

"There's been word from the garrison on the river," Miz Marshall said delicately, still smiling as though we talked of the weather. "It seems some Confederate brass will be visiting, and of course entertainment is required."

Entertainment always meant women, somehow.

"I thought you might like to earn a little extra coin," Miz Marshall concluded. "Fixing up some of the girls' dresses and such. Arranging their hair so nicely. What do you say, Miss Bess?"

Folk had been coming around to ask Maria such things the whole of my life. It wasn't quite talked about, her little nothings; no one outside our home would've known to call them that. But the stamp of her hand was everywhere in Sawgrass, once you knew to look—on babies' heads, twined around with a birthing knot, or newlyweds' thresholds, covered by tokens of love and safety. Somehow, without me much noticing, the work of my own hands had begun to stretch beyond my fingers.

I wasn't sure I liked that, but for now Miz Marshall was gazing at me, waiting. I nodded. "Yes ma'am."

"Like as not you could keep earning it," she said. All that time her voice hadn't risen or changed, yet I heard her above the men's chatter clear as the church bell. "A pretty girl like you."

She didn't mean by the wit of my fingers, or at least not them holding needle and thread.

"Anything else you need, Miz Marshall?" I said, lifting her cup, but my words were drowned in a burst of noise from the door. I leaned past her to see who'd come in, whether it was Pa and Aaron back from the stable and permitting my escape upstairs.

It was—but the three men whose horses were now surely fed and watered in their stalls accompanied them, and the sight of the strangers chilled my blood, for they wore the Confederates' gray and their eyes were on Miz Marshall and me.

CHAPTER FIVE

RAIN HAD COME DURING the night, and the morning arrived dewy and glittering, a touch cooler than the day before. I went out early to do the washing-up, my armfuls of linens taller and bigger around than I was. Ma would be happy if the sheets were hung up to dry before breakfast, and the rain barrels were full of clean water to do them with. The sounds of the inn's yard at daybreak settled around me, driving off the gloom that had hung in my mind since Jonnie's trip to the coast. Never mind what the Confederate men were up to in the garrison, or the Union men at the fort, or the trappers riding out to rustle cattle and smuggle casks of rum between bales of cotton on their barges. Never mind that Jonnie had been asleep in her bed, snoring off Maria's heal-all, by the time I'd gotten upstairs yesterday evening—never mind that I still didn't know what she'd seen on the road from Fort Leon, and never mind that this new gap in my head was steadily filling with outlandish and terrifying scenes.

Somebody had to do the chores, and that body was me.

By the time the sun had fully risen I was stringing the last of the pillowcases to the wash-line. Between damp and twisting white sheets, I saw Jonnie in the paddock at the back of our stable, where land met creek. My hands paused with the clothespin basket. Her trousers were already muddy, which meant the bay limey colt she was training had dumped her at least once. She stood still as he circled her, digging at the dirt with a forehoof.

"Bess!" Ma's voice broke my concentration, and I turned. She stood in the kitchen doorway with a plate in her hands. "Let that be and eat something, sweetheart."

As I came beneath the lean-to, she lifted the plate, gesturing with it. "And save a biscuit for Jonnie, what time she leaves off tormenting that beast."

"She's not tormenting him," I said through a mouthful of cornbread. "You know she doesn't train them that way. With whippings and such." Both sets of our eyes went to the paddock and the figures inside it. Jonnie was astride the bay again, her long legs tight around his skinny barrel. "She'll gentle him down."

"Whipping, gentling—" Ma scoffed, her round face disapproving. "They belong to be in the wild, never mind what Jonnie or anyone else can do to 'em." She startled as the limey reared, her arms going around my shoulders. More than five years we'd had limerunners in the yard, in their pen, and Ma hadn't ever grown accustomed. "You go tell her to eat something and then see to the warmbloods. Your pa and Aaron are off to the docks."

I swallowed a strip of bacon from the plate, then stooped to pet Rex's head where the hound poked out from behind Ma's skirt. "And I suppose this old boy's the only man between us and harm? Eh, laddy?"

"What harm you think might show up…" Ma muttered, but her face only grew stormier. "Go on, then. Both of you."

She'd been in a foul mood for a week and more, it seemed. Ever since we'd returned from the market at Sawyer.

Rex followed as I took the plate toward the paddock fence. He stayed by my feet when I stopped to balance the plate on a post. He didn't bark, and I didn't yell, for fear of startling the bay with Jonnie on his back. We waited until she swung him around in a light canter, the pair of them loping by, and then I raised my arm. She didn't give any sign she'd seen me, but gradually the bay's stride slowed and his circles grew smaller, and finally Jonnie pulled him up. She didn't slide down right away, but took a hand off his neck and lifted her hat.

"What do you think, Bess?"

"Legs 'most as long as yours!" I called back. He looked like a racer to me, but I was no expert. All I knew was the man buying the bay and the gray filly had told Jonnie something specific, and she wouldn't surrender the pair to him until she was satisfied. "Why don't you bring those legs over here?"

My words were light, but my heart ached as I watched her. She seemed whole, moving natural and easy, no sign that either her ribs or her arm were bothering her. Maria's concoctions and stitches were holding her together. All the same, I feared gangrene setting in, what with our hideous heat and damp, or limey poison spreading through her, so soft and subtle she wouldn't notice. She was too danged dreamy sometimes; folk peered at us and thought I must be the fool-girl, small hands and elaborate curls, but Jonnie needed looking after.

And if Maria wouldn't do it to my specifications, maybe I'd have to do it myself.

Jonnie chuckled at me from across the yard, the sweet sound lost to a clatter of hoofbeats on the road out front. The bay snorted, tossing his head with a snap of his jaws. Jonnie walked away from him with her back to me, moving slow and steady, her shadow tall on the dirt. It was never smart to turn your back on them if you could help it. She was closing the stockade gate when voices grew loud on the other side of the barn.

"Well, if you'd just—Elizabeth!" Ma sounded annoyed, more so than she had just a few moments ago. She hurried after two men in gray, strands of hair blowing loose from her bun. "Bess, I done told these gentlemen there weren't anything to see back here, if they're wanting to trade horses they can visit Mr. Boatwright, but—"

They didn't look local—pale skin crackling with sunburn, better fed than anyone I knew—and they didn't sound it either, the moment the taller of the two opened his mouth.

"We hear your Negro girl's the one to see about horses," he said, a heavy twang in his voice. He stared at Jonnie without even a glance at me.

"Why sir," I said, "surely if the military's in need of mounts, that's why there's a—now what's the fellow's name?" I smiled at him, hoping he'd leave Jonnie alone. "The quartermaster?"

The quartermaster or whoever he was could procure them horses, or Jim Boatwright and Rafael Suarez, the two trappers in the area likeliest to have a string to trade, but we all knew the sort of horses these men were after.

"Ain't talking to you, girl." The man's pale eyes didn't leave Jonnie's face except to comb over the rest of her, starting with her muddy boots and ending on her hands as she brushed them together, dirty nails scraping a callus. "Now, that hellbeast in there. It broke for riding?"

Jonnie shrugged. "Not sure who been lying to you, mister, but they're not too trainable."

"Then why you wasting your time with it?"

"Good eating," Jonnie said, face as straight as a rifle shot. "Catch 'em young, feed 'em up nice and fat. Makes a good steak, all right." She got a little closer to the Army man, closer than I liked her, but I had to trust she knew what she was about. It was clear now neither Ma nor I could dissuade the Rebs. "Makes a nice jerky too, you dry the meat out long enough. Could be you'll need something, if the rations get hard."

The angry color of Ma's face drained away to near-white beneath her leathered skin.

The tall man laughed. His companion, squat and compact as an old oak stump Pa and Buck had never been able to drag free of the inn's front drive, didn't even smile. He stood still, not looking at Jonnie or me or even Ma, only at the bay limey pawing about his business inside the paddock.

"High talk for a slave-born kitten," the tall man said. "They do say the ladies of Sawgrass have sharp claws." He reached out and tugged the tail of Jonnie's braid. "That gingery beauty upstairs left her mark on me last night. Hardwick, what do you say?"

The stout man blinked. "Them races they hold over in Sawyer. Sounds to me like somebody trained up those water horses for riding." He looked at Jonnie too now, not the ugly glance of his compatriot but steely-slow, his eyes like a lizard's. "Our Confederacy has the coffers to make any horse trainer rich." He set his hand on the stockade gate. "Now tell me, girl. Should I go in there, would the beast savage me?"

"Could be," Jonnie said.

At my feet, Rex tensed, a snarl coming up from behind his teeth. I crouched to pet him. Nothing needed to be setting these men off, not even an old hunting hound.

"And you'd not prevent it," the stout man said. It wasn't a question. They both had to know no black girl, free or slave, bore them any love. "Tell me how it'd kill me, Miss Jonnie Bruner."

Jonnie's nostrils flared, but she said nothing.

"Them big teeth," he went on, and his head cocked as the bay sidled up inside the paddock, morning sun glinting off his warm coat. "Is it like dogs? They go for the throat, huh?"

"Heard tell of folk fightin' 'em like dogs," the tall man offered. He grinned at me and clicked his own teeth together. Behind his back I saw Ma cross herself, an old movement that felt strange, for I hadn't seen her do so in years. "That right, missy? You two little beauties lying to us? This inn here, must take a pretty penny to run. You get some extra coin on your back, or your pa hold fights with these beasts for folk to bet on?"

There were people around who fought limeys the way others did dogs or cocks, but Pa sure wasn't one of them. I remembered my joke to Ma about Rex keeping us from harm, and wished Pa and Aaron back from the docks.

"We're in the market," the stout man said. His face was hungry now, staring at the limerunner like Jonnie had done a good job talking up the potential for steaks. Then he nodded to Ma. "Let us make you rich, ma'am, or we'll be obliged to make someone else so."

It should've sounded like a tempting offer for a hard-working woman in the southern Florida wastes. Instead I heard it for what it was: a threat.

My candle flickered, its flame blazing and shrinking, the light painting shadows across Jonnie's cheeks. She looked solemn in the dimness of our room, her eyes steady on the cloth beneath my hands.

"Can you fix it, Bess?" she said, as she had the day before in the kitchen, but softer now, hesitant. "I hate to think I ruined it. I know what it cost you. And all for…"

Her voice trailed away, and she shook her head. Her hand moved from where it lay by her side on the window seat and began unwinding strands of her braid. Maybe it was just a trick of candlelight, but it seemed that her fingers trembled.

I kept one eye on my sewing and the other on her. "Tell me what it was like, Jonnie. What happened."

I had my own ideas of how she'd come upon the trappers on the highway—my dreams last night had been full of them, bloody and dark—but I wanted to hear her version. I'd never be able to bear it, her doing what she intended, if she didn't at least talk to me about it.

Snipping a thread, I added, "And tell me what you— what you saw."

"What was I supposed to do?" She dragged both hands through her hair now and bent her head, leaving the tendrils loose and blanketing as the Seminole people did when they mourned. "Them Northerners, how long have they known war was coming? What use is there anymore in these messages they send back and forth when the Rebs are so bald about it? Those two this morning—" She scoffed. "The whole countryside will know the Confederates aim to use limeys for their battles, they're not bothering to hide it."

"Some folk will sell to them," I said, completing a row of neat stitches across the inside of the velvet jacket's sleeve. I'd made them as tiny as I knew how, and now the sleeve would have to be steamed and re-draped, for velvet didn't take to a simple patch, and then I'd sew it back onto the jacket's body. "I can see the glint in Jim Boatwright's eye already. His string'll be dangling loose 'fore any of us can blink."

Trappers would sell anything to anyone, that was known. They'd make no bones about bartering with the Rebs, only money doing so. It didn't matter whether Confederate greed would bear fruit; by the time anyone knew whether you really could use limeys as war mounts, the water horses would be wiped out. The trappers would sell any limerunner already captured, and they'd sell any skills they had at catching the horses and breaking them, and someone—so it seemed—had already sold the information that Jonnie was the best around at that game.

A small curl of fire seemed to leap from the candle and embed itself in my chest.

"I loathe to feel helpless," Jonnie whispered. She looked at me through her hair, eyes huge. "I'm not helpless. Those bastards—they don't know what they're in for. I'll show 'em, by hell."

I gazed down at the sleeve lying across my lap. No matter how well I shaped it, I'd always know the gash was there, where a trapper's knife had caught Jonnie's arm. Three inches south and it would've been buried in her ribs: a boar knife, a mean little crescent better used for shelling crabs, a double-bladed Bowie. I couldn't decide which injury pained me more, the one inflicted by a human she hated or the one she'd received from an animal she loved.

"Which bastards do you mean? Slavers or Rebs?"

"Same thing, aren't they?" She laughed a little and got up from the window seat and sat down again, legs folded, on my bed. "I see trappers with human cargo, I'll do what I can. I see Rebs pressing men into service or rounding up limeys to fight—oh, believe me, I'll—"

A hand crept over my knee. She sucked in her breath, fingers pinching at the fabric of my nightgown. "Bess, there were three of 'em and I didn't even think, I didn't stop, I barely felt Keke under me. She was flying. I believe I heard her laugh when she bit one of those men. Do you think horses can laugh?"

If horses laughed, warmblood or limey or unicorn out of fairy stories, Jonnie would know.

"And when it was done, I saw…" Something in my chest hitched at her words, the sudden flash of her face burning bright as the moon with awe. "I swear I saw her, Bess. Right there in the road in front of me."

"Her? Who, Keke?"

Jonnie's fingers tensed around my knee. Her lips moved silently once, as though in prayer. Then she said, "Ada Nuit. I saw her. I swear it was her."

Ada Nuit. The Maroon goddess, slaves' queen, lady of the roads and marshways, a legend known only to our parts and not one I'd ever thought on much, just another feature of the swamp and prairie—and Jonnie had seen her?

"Who else, Bess? Tall and pale as lightning," Jonnie said. Her voice dipped so low I barely caught it, like she was afraid to speak the vision out loud for the walls to hear and the owls outside to bear away. "Right in front of me at the fork where the Leon road goes inland, big as the trees, and her troop everywhere around me. I was afeared I'd be caught on the corpse road, but they just swarmed around her while she looked at me."

The notion of a ghostly queen looking at Jonnie with her more-than-dead eyes chilled me to the bone.

"She nodded," Jonnie whispered. "And—and she laughed, that I know. Maybe Keke can't laugh, but Ada Nuit laughed and then they all rode away." She sighed, a wisp of breath catching my curls aflutter. "All I could think… all I felt was that it was right. I was right to set on those trappers and help the people get loose of them. We followed Ada Nuit's troop straight to Haasi Town, Bess. Like it was what she wanted."

It knocked me sideways, the fervor in her voice. Her eyes looked like those of the priest, the few times we'd snuck into Mass to watch the tiny service.

"You reckon they'd back me?" she asked. "The Union men? If I could get them goods—money, maybe…"

"Like Robin Hood," I said, voice faraway as I struggled to collect myself. One of the few books in the house besides the Bible was a volume of old tales, full of the knights Jonnie loved and tales of little people under the hill, and a bandit who stole from evil, rich men to help the poor.

Jonnie giggled. When I looked at her again, her cheeks were warm and she seemed more herself. "Maybe you ought to make me a green jacket, Miss Elizabeth the Light-fingered, and a cap to match."

"Red is your color," I said primly, holding up the sleeve so she could see the repairs. "It's both of us our color."

She looked not at the sleeve but at me, long and unblinking, until heat rose in my face too.

"There," she said, smiling a little, "so it is."

Her hand moved from my knee to my shoulder, and then my throat, until her palm was nestled in my hair, cupped to my cheek. "Bess. You believe me, don't you? You understand?"

Our faces were close, loose tendrils of her hair tickling my skin. Her fingers tugged a few braids I'd left in mine, and my heart hammered in my chest, fear and love mingled. The Confederate men who'd come to see about the limeys had not left my mind, and now there was the matter of Ada Nuit sticking her ghoulish nose in people's business. No matter what Jonnie thought, no matter how vicious Keke could be when she was irked, the Rebs were grown men—not just the Rebs but all of them, the Union Army men and trappers alike, and they had their superiors and brothers behind them, guns and knives and strong horses of their own. She could ride one of the Devil's own mounts and she'd still be a girl, just a girl.

But now, maybe, a girl blessed by a dread queen.

I kissed her. "I understand. Although I think you're pretty convincing even without goddesses from wonder tales appearing to you. What, you think the whole town won't be behind you, when they hear about the glorious fight on the Leon highway?" Her lips moved, a smile against mine. "No love for the Rebs here, why, I'll bet you even Jamie Little and Sol will turn up empty-handed once the Rebs come sniffing around for limeys."

"What do you bet?"

"The last of those tarts your mother made today."

"Or something sweeter," Jonnie murmured. She took the sleeve from my lap and laid it carefully on the trunk we kept near the window. The rest of its jacket was on my dress-form in the corner, waiting to be made whole again. Jonnie stretched out on my narrow bed and tugged until I was gathered against her. The straw-tick and lone feather pillow were too small for the pair of us now, but I had no complaints. Her lips moved gently over my earlobe as she said, "I'll never leave you."

Maybe that wouldn't be up to her.

"I don't know," I said, pretending to be serious lest I started crying. "Now what if I make an honest man out of Sol one of these days?"

Her waist quivered with laughter and I squeezed her, avoiding the bite on her ribs.

"What if I take Warren Almquist's offer to run away on the steamer to Jacksonville?"

"Anyone but Warren." She laughed outright, her head thrown back on the pillow. "Oh, Bess, promise me if there's a man, it's not Warren."

"What if you go out riding one of these nights and the road just catches you up?" Now that her vision was in my mind, I couldn't stop thinking about it. "Ada Nuit led you to Haasi Town, but what if her band swallows you up next time?"

"I'd lead them straight back here again," Jonnie said. Her voice was slower, her giggles gone. I could hear sleep coming over her. I snuggled closer, wrapping my leg through hers, and listened to her breathe. She murmured something more, the words muffled in my hair.

We'd left the window open, but I was too sleepy to get up and close it. Outside, cradled in the panes, the moon rose narrow as a fingernail. An image flashed in my brain, Maria sweeping fingernail parings into the hearth, and curls of hair when she trimmed mine or Jonnie's, admonishing us never to leave bits of ourselves for the taking. There was work to be done on such pieces, and safer if they were burned. Once, on a night even darker than this, in the midst of a winter storm when Ma and Pa and Jonnie were all abed, she'd shown me one such little nothing… how even the smallest bit of a person's self could be caught, how who that person was lived in their spittle and piss, and how simple it was, really, to weave hooks into tiny crevices and wiggle them wide to bursting.

It was a smuggler's moon, that pale sliver, and as sleep took me, I wondered who was riding the roads and waterways tonight, if not Jonnie.

CHAPTER SIX

I KNEW BEFORE I MOVED in the bed that the space next to me, never mind how narrow, was empty.

The muslin sheet was cool when I put my hand out. I couldn't think how Jonnie had gotten out of bed without waking me; it was usual enough, one of us falling asleep in the other's bed and then stumbling into our own during the night. I was something of a greedy sleeper, so I'd been told, and sometimes Jonnie tired of my feet on her legs or my arm around her waist. But the straw-tick across from mine was vacant too, its neat coverlet untroubled.

It was dark in our room yet, between midnight and dawn, but my eyes knew the space well enough to see the velvet jacket on its dress-form, and the loose sleeve lying where Jonnie had left it across the trunk. Her boots were gone, and her belt. I swung my feet onto the braided rug and stood, fumbling for the lamp. Tears stung my eyes. This was going to be it, then: her riding off at all hours when she didn't even have a message to carry. Her and Keke running straight for trouble, and not even with a certain jacket to protect them.

I was halfway down the stairs in my stockings before it occurred to me that I should stop in the front hall where my father kept his guns.

The rifle I picked was one I supposed I could shoot, if things turned that way—if Jonnie needed me to—if I found her and… I stuffed that thought away, checking to be sure shells were already in the chamber. Pa didn't like to leave loaded weapons lying around, but it was faster, what times the trappers got to arguing amongst themselves or with newcomers.

He had made sure Jonnie and I both knew how to shoot, because it was senseless to have girls running around helpless in a country where most anything would try to hurt them at some point. A rattlesnake, a gator, a man. Jonnie was better than me, because she practiced more, went hunting with Pa and messed around with some of the boys from town now and then for shooting contests. With the sale of the first limey she trained, she'd bought a pair of Colt pistols.

Even I had to admit they were beautiful, finely-made and powerful, and she'd made them even lovelier. Sat up with them for several nights, carving their mother-of-pearl handles into rosettes and snakes and skulls, polishing their walnut muzzles with strokes that seemed measured, like a church ritual.

They never left her belt but when she was caring for them. They were weighting her seat on Keke's back even now, out there down the dark road.

I grumbled something mean to myself and went back through the main room. Ma was a good shot herself. A snakeskin hung on the wall next to the mantel, an eight-foot rattler she'd fired on from the kitchen's back door. She hadn't intended on keeping the skin, but Maria had insisted. Hefting the rifle in my hand, I smiled despite things. That was Maria for you. She'd skinned the thing and fried the flesh in long strips and Ma had cracked a grin while chomping on some of it. When Pa tacked the skin up on the wall, Maria nodded approvingly and said that for miles around everyone, folk and animals alike, would know to respect the Ramseys or be consumed by them.

"And what's all this?"

Maria's voice came from the darkened hearth in the kitchen, as though by thinking of her I'd called her straight down out of her bed. I breathed out in a great gush, trying to calm my heart.

"Maria! You think it's smart to startle a gal with a gun?"

"I think you're a little slow on the draw with that thing, missy," she said. She didn't get up from where she sat among baskets of cloth strips. The town loved Maria's braided rugs. The one taking shape on her lap looked to be the colors and knots she used for newlyweds. "Bess, don't lie to me."

"If you're awake I figure you saw her leave."

"I didn't see nothing of the kind." Maria sighed. "You're a nice girl, my Bess, we raised you to use the front door. I suppose Johanna's not so nice, for she drops down out of the window. As well you know."

I frowned. "You're not stopping me?"

"How am I to stop rushing water?" She flapped a strip of red cloth at me. "Your parents don't believe in chaining a girl to her bed and nor do I." She stood and came toward me. Taking the rifle from my hands, she checked the barrel and cocked it. Then her lips pressed my forehead. "You think I don't know what she saw?"

"You mean Ada Nuit."

The name left my throat a whisper. Something in me quailed to speak it loud, even in the dark quiet of the house.

"Ada Nuit," Maria repeated. "*Reine fantome,* that one. They in Haasi Town, they swear to her and the road does too, and all who walk or ride—if Jonnie says—"

Her face glowed as Jonnie's had when she'd described her vision. They both had a fever in them. Jonnie's was usually for all things four-footed, but Maria's was harder to pin down. It flared in her lovely broad cheekbones when she looked on her daughter doing something I would've described as foolish, and sometimes when she and me spoke of our little nothings, the words we wove over our best beloveds, and most often when her husband, Jonnie's father, entered her hearth tales. And now here it was, for a will-o'-the-wisp, a swamp shade leading her daughter—and to where, I was afraid I knew.

"I swam the Sanctus at Hopper Point when I was carrying Jonnie," Maria said. Hopper Point was the widest the river got, so broad you could hardly see the far shore. "Gators I saw and limerunners too, a sea of teeth circling and snapping. I felt like my blood had been drained out and my veins filled with lead, I was so tired. But I saw light on the water, light all along that shore waiting for me, and when I washed up among the Maroons, they said to see a light in the marsh was to see Ada Nuit."

Maria pressed her forehead to mine, her skin cool and smooth. "Her hand has been on Johanna for a long time, my Bess. She carries our girl and now, if she wants something..."

I trembled as she laughed softly. "Go. Make your mistakes."

A whole row of warmbloods poked their heads over their stalls when I came into the barn. The bay limey in his pen would've been faster than any of them, but he wasn't trained yet, and I was no rider of the water horses. Our cart-horse Spots was the most reliable, but getting on in the years. Buck, the draft horse, was unshakable but slow. I had a hankering to borrow Sol Rowland's half-Arab mare, but if I ran her lame or got her shot he'd have my head in his saddlebags before anyone could stop him. I went into the stall where Aaron kept his buckskin and saddled the mare as quick as I knew.

The inn was eerily quiet when I led the buckskin gal up the drive. I knew it inside and out, the exact shapes of the moss-strung oaks and cabbage palms in the dark, the shell-road's crunch beneath my boots. My parents were still asleep in their room on the second floor, and Maria's room was empty. I'd avoided every creaky floorboard in the hall so as not to wake the guests, and it was long past the hour for the girls upstairs to be entertaining said guests. Rex had not howled when I went past him in the breezeway, for he knew me.

All the town knew me, and sometimes it felt all the land did too—sometimes, as now, when the road opened up wide and the skinny moon on the horizon looked like a girl's white smile. That was a good thing, usually, when it was trading time and Jim Boatwright or Mr. Almquist said *carry that along home, Miss Bess, your pa's good for it* because I'd looked a little too long at a fine red ribbon.

I liked Sawgrass and its people, and I liked to be known, to feel as though the place belonged to me. A few of the girls who'd attended Miss Anthorpe's schoolroom envied me, I liked to think, and that was pleasant; just about every boy around envied Jonnie and that was better still. But as the buckskin picked up her feet and I pointed her south, I wished for the night to cover me as my coat did, for its fingers to reach down and pluck Jonnie from harm if harm had found her.

It was better not to be known in our parts; if folk knew you, they could find you.

The men in their gray coats had found Jonnie earlier that morning, and I didn't believe even a little that they'd gone away satisfied. And she was going to keep putting herself in their path. Keep on running right up to them. Keep dangling limeys in front of their pasty noses, then snatching them away—keep freeing those their new government preferred stay bound, and thieve anything worth taking while she was at it, probably.

Beneath me, the buckskin's pace increased, turning from a jog into a gallop, her ears pricked as though she'd heard something that hadn't reached me yet. I didn't know exactly where to head, only the likeliest direction. The feeling that had kicked me downstairs to grab a rifle and snatch a horse boiled beneath my ribs, a confused churn like fish thrashing in a shallow pond.

I wished Maria had tried a little harder to keep me back.

The sounds came to me before the sight of those who made them.

My heart leapt up in my throat, terror spurred by shouts and hoofbeats, and I kicked at the buckskin mare. She was already galloping faster than I knew how to ride, but I was still on her back and I wouldn't let her leave me in the dust until I saw Jonnie with my own eyes. It had to be her up ahead, for who else would it be? We were too far from the garrison for any of the Rebels' goings-on to be audible, if they ever conducted exercises past midnight. This part of the highway between Sawgrass and the coast was quiet, the sandy road splitting at a fork and then narrowing until a man could stand in the middle and touch the trees on either side.

Of course, that meant one man could hold the road if he had a mind to. One man… or one girl.

She and Keke were riding straight down the road south of the fork that led into Sawgrass proper, across Sanctus Creek, and in front of them—between road and bridge—sat a wagon. I leaned down into the buckskin's mane and grabbed up her reins, slowing her. When she was moving at a fast jog, I swung my father's rifle up to my shoulder and tried to figure why the wagon wasn't moving. It was a shadow in a landscape of shadows, its bulk outlined against the water beyond, and the horses hitched to it were berserking. Wherever their driver was, he wasn't making any effort to control them, drive them away from Jonnie and toward the bridge.

Then I realized the bridge over the Sanctus was missing.

It was only a narrow row of planks, but it was necessary: the creek couldn't be forded at that point, not because it was so deep but because it was full of rocks, big boulders just beneath the water that kicked up the current and made it impossible for wagons to pass. Jonnie had somehow dismantled the planks and trapped the wagon.

The buckskin slowed further, shying to the roadside, and I knew she'd caught Keke's scent. That was likely the cause of the wagon's horses going moonwise too; warm-bloods didn't cotton to limeys. They knew, somewhere back in their instincts, that a water horse would savage them even if they were kin—that limeys turned canni-bal when driven to starvation, or even when they were feeling particularly ornery. The dank, wet scent of them wasn't my favorite, but warm-blooded horses hated it. I struggled with the mare, urging her forward, as a flash lit up the night.

The wagon's driver had fired, and done a poor job of it, because Keke was still pelting down the road. Answering flares sparkled against the trees, and some-one yelled. And then Keke was pulling up, her forelegs kicking as she reared and plunged down again, and the figure on her back leaned out of the saddle. I ducked my head toward the rifle on my shoulder, just in time to miss the blade of Jonnie's machete meeting flesh. The wagon's driver screamed, or maybe that was Keke, a drawn-out keen that raised the hair along the nape of my neck. The buckskin whinnied and bolted, and I clung to her one-handed, dragging at the reins to turn her before she carried me away from Jonnie entirely.

The body sprawled on the sand didn't look to be getting up any time soon, but another shape jumped from the wagon, dashing between the pair of horses still tangled in their traces. Wan light from the setting moon caught a blade, its slashing movement aimed at Keke's legs. I fired without thinking about it.

The shot didn't hit. It did startle the second person such that a hoof caught them broadside—one of their own horse's too, not Keke's. That didn't stop Keke from stepping on the person once they were down on the sand with their fellow.

"Well," Jonnie said when I reined the buckskin alongside her, keeping a tight grip on the mare's mouth. "Damnation. What are you doing out here?"

"What are *you*?" I cried. "How did you—the bridge—did you—?"

I was not my most eloquent when flustered.

Her teeth appeared. "Not a bad shake, hey? I always wanted to try that."

I wanted to reach over and shake her, myself.

"Ever since Rafael told me he held up some cattlemen from driving their herd over the bridge," she went on, blasé as the day was long, like there weren't two men bleeding at her feet. "Worked a trick, huh?"

"I just…" I let the buckskin back up a few steps, for Keke was eyeing us with a look in her blue peeper that I didn't like at all. "We need to get back home. Take whatever you were aiming for and let's get away from here. We can come back and fix the bridge tomorrow."

"Think we can manage the horses between us?" Jonnie said, casting a glance at the wagon's pair. They'd calmed somewhat, now that the loud noises had ceased, but their eyes rolled at Keke, and I could hear their breath wet and labored. "Maybe we can hitch yours in and you drive."

"The whole wagon," I muttered. "Of course. What on earth's in this thing that you're wanting it so bad?"

"Goddamn," one of the men on the sand gasped. He was curled over on himself, clutching his side where a dark blot spread over his vest. He coughed and spat more blood at Keke. "You sneaky little—some kind of traitor, is that it? Damned darkie bitch."

Jonnie didn't voice a command to Keke, and I didn't even see her hands move on the limey's mane, but Keke's right foreleg kicked out. After that the man was still.

The other man was facedown, for a body didn't get up quick from a hoof to the head. I couldn't tell if he was breathing.

"Munitions," Jonnie said, her voice quiet. "The Union men at the fort want the schedule for supply trains, Sol said. So I figured I'd follow them a bit, but…" She patted Keke's neck, then slid down from her back. "They're carting a cannon along, Bess. I spied gun crates too. I'd a heap rather the Rebs at the garrison never get those supplies in the first place."

I swallowed against a dry throat. Two men dead in front of me was a shake-up to be sure, and I wasn't certain it wasn't quite a sin, even if they were treasonous slavers. But the ache in my chest was all for Jonnie. She stood there, cool as you please, but my mind couldn't believe she was whole. I wouldn't believe it until I'd touched her, checked her ribs and legs and eyes, held her close as could be.

Keeping the reins wound in one hand, I dismounted from the buckskin. Jonnie looked up from where she was seeing to the wagon horses, and her face softened. Her head tipped against mine when I wrapped my free arm around her. "Ah, Bess, don't you fret. We're here and they're not, and what more can you say?"

"You shouldn't've—" I started, my eyes blurring. She was too thin in my hands. She'd always been lean, tall and rangy, but ever since she'd started catching limeys she'd worked too hard, not eaten enough. I wanted to stow her away in our room and let Maria feed her for at least a week, no stopping. "You went riding without your jacket, Jonnie."

"No message to send tonight," she whispered back. "I wasn't going to the coast, just up the road."

"I don't care! I don't care whether I sew in a message or not." Now I did shake her, clutching her fast and then pushing her away. "I'll fix that sleeve up and then you wear it. You always wear that jacket. Promise me."

"I promise," she said, but there was a question in her voice.

"I can't do nothing else for you," I said. "Least I can do is sew you up. Tie off all the threads. Make sure…"

My voice broke entirely, and a sob clawed at my lungs. Keke danced away from the sound, but Jonnie pulled me close again. She took the hand unoccupied with reins and put it to her cheek.

"I'm all right. I'm here, see me?" I made myself nod, my face in her hair. She nestled my hand between us so I could feel her heartbeat. "I'm alive and I aim to stay that way." I nodded again, and she kissed the bend of my neck, the only bit of me visible between hair and dress. "You sure helped me stay that way. Shooting on this fellow like that."

"I won't do it again."

A lie, but it asserted itself something pitiful, as though I could convince both of us that I'd ever stop trying to keep her safe.

"Wouldn't ask you to," Jonnie said. She laughed softly. "I'm only saying thank you." Her fingers tangled in mine, nudging between my breasts. "You're a sight with a rifle in your hands, Miss Elizabeth Ramsey, I'll tell you."

She was a sight with a machete, or her pistols, the matched set hooked to her belt and jutting against my hip. Oh, she was a sight even in plain trousers and a dark coat just now, never mind her fancy scarlet jacket and the collar I'd sewn for her. That collar, French-stitched as dainty as I could manage, and how I'd dreamed she'd wear it to a church dance or the next market day, fine and lovely beside me... how I'd known it would gleam against her brown skin above that goddamned jacket. Despite everything—the death on the ground nearby, the weapons of war in the wagon—I was hungry for her. My eyes fell on her like I'd never seen her before, and my hands were greedy.

"I promise," she said again, lower. "I got a thing to do and I know I'll see it through. Your jacket will help me. I swear it, Bess. On Ada Nuit."

I could've stood there all night with her, reassuring myself that she hadn't left me, reveling in the thrill of her in the dark, casting a shadow even at midnight. That shadow would grow, I knew, as word of this spread. What time the Rebs found their men on the road tomorrow or the next day, fear would spring up ahead of Keke's hooves. The half-myth of Jonnie riding with the Queen of Corpses would blaze like wildfire through Sawgrass. That was all her doing, daring and stubborn and irresistible, beautiful in her velvet and lace.

I'd never be full of her.

CHAPTER SEVEN

ONCE I'D WATCHED A blacksmith in town make wire. She was a brawny woman who'd taken over the business of crafting nails and horseshoes and hoes after her brother died. He'd been kicked in the head while shoeing a horse, a fact that fascinated Jonnie and horrified me. It was too easy to imagine her on the dirt, blood darkening her braids and the vivid color slowly draining from her skin while one of the creatures she loved ran wild.

Nonetheless, I snuck off with Jonnie when she had a mind to mosey into town and look things over, and one of her favorite stops was the smith. That day the woman had been drawing wire to make fences, pulling long sheets of iron through a board with holes in it until they ran narrower and narrower. She didn't talk much, the smith, but she told us that you could make any wire that way, just the metal and the holes, everything from the thicker gauge she was making into sharp-edged fence to delicate silver-washed loops used for jewelry.

Irene's hair reminded me of the finest wire as I braided it, like black gold. Night-deep, darker than Jonnie's and curly with it, coils tight and tiny and even, so lovely my plans for her braids had changed as I began making them. She sighed and wriggled under my hands. "Bess, you must be near about done. Speed it up, would you?"

"If you keep still, I'll be done before you can blink."

She wasn't particularly good at keeping still. Nervy as a colt, was Irene, and the word went that that held true in the upstairs rooms when men visited her—that she was bossy, she had to be in charge.

I hoped some of her sauce stayed with her tonight, when the girls rode with Miz Marshall to the garrison. That hope went into the plaits between my fingers as I tied them off with slender blue ribbons: that she wouldn't let the Rebel men boss her, but that her tongue wouldn't get her into trouble, neither. There was a tension in all the little nothings Maria and I whispered and wove. The best parts of a person had to be upheld... and the parts that could bring them to harm were muffled, muted for a time.

I counted them all off, the girls who worked in the inn and another wayhouse closer to Sawgrass, and now and again the hostel in Sawyer. They adorned me and Jonnie's room like jewels themselves this evening, sparkling in finery that seemed far too lovely to waste on

Confederates. Their assorted beauties and charms seemed new to my eyes tonight; their closeness, their scents and twitches and glances kicked up a turmoil in my stomach as I worked.

Anne had put her face close to mine and near begged me to soften the high temper that went with her red hair. I didn't mind such requests coming from one I knew well—Anne had been part of my life for long years. Diffused into many small braids, her quickness to anger became beckoning and seduction, woven through intricate herringbones running down her back like water lit by sunset.

But then Marta had murmured in her shifty English for me to *braid me beauty, Bess*, and I wondered who watched me at work when I thought all in the dining room was calm, who'd heard aught of my fingers beyond the embroidered hangings decorating the inn. How should she know else? I held my tongue and put my hands on her blond hair. Truthfully she wasn't much to look at, and needed what beauty I could gift her. I'd threaded her hair into a large fisherman's knot and caught it up in a sheer, glimmering net so that she might catch attention, catch coins, catch gossip more than she already had.

Cassie's square face and schoolmarm manner of talking were softened by loose, thick coils low on her neck, tendrils left to twist around her temples, suddenly coy. I was grateful, so grateful it shamed me, when she only thanked me and slipped me a coin for a tip.

Meg, the youngest and no one could figure out why she was in this neighborhood of business when she seemed to fear men—but I'd wound her chestnut locks into a towering crown, one thick base braid set off by several slim plaits twisted through one another, and prayed some commanding presence into them. She'd said nothing as I worked, her eyes fast on mine in the mirror.

And then came Irene, haughty Irene, prettier than anyone around except Jonnie, and wasn't that its own weapon, as well as its own doom?

"Bess," Anne said as she drew on short lace gloves. I drew breath in turn, bracing myself for what might come out of her mouth. "That collar you made for Jonnie. Couldn't I beg one off you? I'll owe you." She batted her eyes at me. "I'll give you a kiss."

"Kisses return no interest," I said primly, relieved, though I was already designing a lace collar in my mind, a frosty white confection to set off her freckled skin and blue eyes. Patting Irene's shoulder, I added, "There. Now get away from me with your wiggles."

Irene turned, admiring herself in the mirror. Braids covered the crown of her head, a jagged pattern Maria had taught me. It came from her mother's people, all the way from the Horn of Africa, carried across the ocean and sent down the American coast on the heads of women. Her curls fanned out below the plaits, a black cloud soft on her bare shoulders.

"Well enough," she sniffed. I smothered a grin behind my hand. "I don't see why Miz Marshall made you do all this, Bess. They're just men. Can't expect a bunch of traitor sailors to admire such handiwork."

"Miz Marshall wants you all looking your best," I said, blithe and careless as I could manage. If she'd not heard yet what Maria's hands might achieve, what mine had put into the girls' braids tonight, I wasn't going to tell her just as she sailed off into a viper nest. "You know as well as anybody that a man might not take note of the particulars, but he's sure affected by the whole pretty picture."

The girls giggled, a murmur of gossip rising up as they adjusted petticoats and necklines. They were never short of observations about the men of Sawgrass and the trappers alike, their handsomeness or otherwise, their proclivities, their secrets. Irene alone watched me in the mirror, eyes narrowed.

"You're looking rather pretty yourself, Miss Elizabeth. Got somewhere to be?"

I did look pretty, I admitted to myself modestly; I'd done my own hair up in my favorite style, parted straight down the center and combed smooth, just tight enough to keep it in place but loose enough to drape coquettishly over my cheek when I turned my head. It was caught beneath my chin into a fat braid, the end of which coiled up and pinned, invisible, at the nape of my neck. A red ribbon curved throughout, a flicker in the darkness drawn into a rosette over my left ear, and with each stroke of my hairbrush, each twist of my fingers, I'd woven in a sort of deflection. A sliding of the eye, like a stone skipping across water. Pretty, but not so pretty anyone would want me in their hand. I hadn't forgotten what Miz Marshall had offered me that morning not so many days ago, how she'd looked at me assessingly, as though I was a pig at the livestock fair.

It was always better to have a knife in hand, whatever shape that knife took.

"Miz Marshall asked Jonnie to drive," I said by way of explanation. "I thought I'd come along, keep her from falling asleep out of boredom while y'all do business."

After our adventure at the Sanctus bridge, I wasn't about to let her out of my sight after dark if I could help it.

Irene *hmmed* disapprovingly as Jonnie came through the door, right on cue. "Miz Marshall says you need to get downstairs. Nearly sunset." She held up her hands when Irene bumped by her, not bothering to try to keep her bustle out of the way. "Lord a'mighty—I'm just delivering the message."

Irene's curls disappeared down the stairs in a flounce. The rest of the girls trailed after her, Anne tipping me a wink. Everyone thought Irene and Jonnie didn't get on because Irene was heartbroken over my mislaid affections. Even if that was true—doubtful—she would've had plenty of warning. Never had I loved anyone but Jonnie, not since we were children, and Irene had only arrived in Sawgrass to ply her trade but some months prior.

"Bess," Jonnie said. She was plainest of all of us in her everyday trousers and boots, having let me convince her that wearing her red jacket right into a Rebel stronghold was maybe not the brightest idea anyone had ever had. "No reason for you to ride along. It isn't safe."

"What care had you for safety last night?" I cuddled up close to her on the landing outside our bedroom. "Seems a good bit safer to pile into a wagonful of ladies on whom no one would wish harm than to go riding down a gun shipment in the middle of the night."

"Those two who came about the limeys," Jonnie went on. Her lips were tight, sad. I wanted to kiss them into some happier shape. "For certain they'll be at the garrison. I heard tell one was a commander—the stout one, with those ugly eyes. Christ mercy, I didn't like his eyes, Bess." Her arm slid around my waist. "I hate to think of you near 'em."

I hated to think of her anywhere in the same county as those two. I didn't fear their desires as men; that was Miz Marshall's business and that of the girls, not mine. I surely feared their desires as military officers with a goal in mind. They could have any girl they sought, and those women prettier than me, but Jonnie was singular and far more valuable.

Well, better we were together, whatever happened on the road or inside the garrison's walls.

The garrison's gates closed behind us just as Okeechobee swallowed the sun.

It wasn't a fort of size, like Leon at the coast, coquina-girt and worthy of a real name. The walls were oak fortified with an outer ring of sharpened pine stakes, and the buildings within just a scrabble of tents, lean-tos, barracks, and a large central cabin that served as the camp's headquarters.

Before the United States had rent itself in two, the Army men in the garrison liked to believe their location on the Sanctus gave them control of the river and its traffic, commerce and smuggling alike. Every trapper in Sawgrass environs knew better. The Nag's Head was often thick with laughter and derision over which trapper's vessel had escaped notice that night.

Florida was lawless, so it went, and our part perhaps more so than most. Being situated in the convergence of ocean, river, and lake meant that we saw every kind of movement, from deer stalking the scrub to buccaneers sailing inland from the coast and escaped slaves running south from the Georgia border. I didn't envy the constables their duties of maintaining peace and order, not that they'd ever seemed too adept at it.

Nor did I have any pity to spare for the sailors now populating its stockade as the wagon trundled through their encampment.

I couldn't recall a time when the garrison hadn't been stationed on the banks of the Sanctus, but still it struck my eye like a scar across smooth flesh. It was made uglier now by the flag flying above headquarters, a barred square of red flapping in the warm night breeze, a reminder to all who looked on it that the men and weapons inside the garrison were Rebels, involuntary conscripts at best and man-hunting traitors at worst.

Jonnie spat to the side as she drew the wagon up outside headquarters. Miz Marshall, perched tall and straight on the seat next to her, made no comment on her behavior. Jonnie looked at her, and then over her shoulder at all of us in the wagon bed, a nest of ruffles and ribbons and braids.

"It's cruel," she said to Miz Marshall, low, beneath the girls' chatter. "Bringing Irene here to these—" Her throat worked, a hard swallow against what I knew she wanted to say. "They'll not treat a girl like her with any kindness, should they even look at her."

Jonnie's words fell like hail on my ears, though I didn't think Irene had heard her. Black girls who worked as Irene did had to be careful of white men. Everyone knew the use white slave-owners gave their female chattel, and a bunch of Rebels in a fort were worse, surely.

"I agree," Miz Marshall said calmly. "I never give a woman reason to call me cruel." Her lips were quite red this evening, their color no doubt heightened with some cosmetic. Maria didn't approve of such things, and Ma always pinched my cheeks and told me I didn't need them. "Anne, Meg, Marta, and Cassie are due inside, what time the men permit us entrance. Irene has another assignation waiting for her."

It came to me again, that no one exactly knew the extent and details of Miz Marshall's business.

The headquarters door opened and a square of yellow light appeared, spilling laughter and conversation and a clatter of boots. Several figures moved toward the wagon.

"Ladies!" a voice called. A man stopped next to Miz Marshall, removing his hat as he looked up at her. "Welcome. We're pleased to make you comfortable inside, if you'll follow."

I squinted as the girls began climbing out of the wagon bed, trying to see into the headquarters cabin. Men moved about behind the waxed-paper windows; I heard the clink of dice and bottles, and a colorful scattering of cards flickered into view as window papers rustled in the breeze. Gradually the gray uniforms were softened by low bodices and ruffled sleeves and lace-covered fingers toying with lapels and locks of hair.

A hand grasped my upper arm, jerking my attention from the windows. "Get hopping, missy," said the man who'd come to fetch the girls.

"I believe you're mistaken, sir," I said, trying to smile. I was already rattled by the drive. All through the countryside I'd kept seeing points of light at the sides of my eyes, and visions of Ada Nuit's ghost troop danced in my head. "Why, I'm just—" I remembered Irene. "We're chaperoning these girls, no more."

Chaperone was a silly word for a seventeen-year-old, given that Marta was nearly ten years my senior and Anne another five beyond that, but the man's leer chilled my bones. I didn't know why Irene wasn't moving, but I wasn't too keen on letting the man move her himself.

"That's the last of them," Miz Marshall said, her voice low and calm. "If you'd be so kind?"

"Pity," the man said. He gave me another glance, ran his tongue over his teeth and grinned. "You're too pretty to leave behind. Good gold waiting for you, girl. Won't you come in with us?"

Good gold indeed. Worthless Confederate scrip, like as not. I smoothed my skirt over my knees and pressed my shoulders into the wagon's seat, holding my face serene. I wanted him to go away with Miz Marshall, and I wanted Jonnie to stay put, not pull anything dangerous, not throw herself between me and him.

Miz Marshall's hand on the man's arm seemed formed of iron. After a moment of her digging her nails in and smiling at him, he scoffed and bore Miz Marshall to the headquarters door with an exaggerated bow. Beside me, Irene blew out her breath.

"Well! Now that's all done—Jonnie, would you mind moving these nags?"

"What exactly are you here for?" Jonnie snapped. "Miz Marshall didn't tell me nothing like that, only that you all was driving over here to keep the Rebs happy and would I care to accompany?" She patted the rifle in its socket on the wagon's side. "Seeing as you never know when you might need a fair shot."

"I'd rather you didn't drag us all into a firefight," Irene said right back. "Pull over to the south corner. Tonight, if you please?"

"South corner," Jonnie muttered, and something else after for which Maria would've scrubbed her tongue with a brush, but she slapped the reins and let the horses jog across the garrison toward the far corner of the stockade wall.

A small building squatted there, tucked right up against the boards, and a figure stood nonchalantly against its wall. A hand stretched out to Buck's nose when Jonnie drew the horses up, and I realized it was someone familiar. Sol Rowland's brown beard and fancy checked vest slid briefly into torchlight and again into shadow.

"Miss Irene, you better step pretty or you'll miss them."

Irene was out of the wagon-bed in a rustle of petticoats and a last hostile glance at Jonnie. She reached up to pat my elbow. "Thank you for the braids, Bess. I'm proud to look so nice tonight."

"Where—" I hissed after her. "Irene!"

But she was gone, her blue skirt fluttering between gaps in the fence as Sol held a board to the side. I frowned, trying to see around him, but there was nothing beyond dark woods and the faint glitter of water.

"All right," Jonnie whispered, her voice hushed but fierce. "What's all this, Sol?"

"Suarez's cutter is headed down to the Tortugas," Sol said quietly. "There's a boat bound for Cuba after that. Did you know Irene is a runaway?"

"Well," Jonnie said. "Sure."

I hadn't known that, exactly, but it wasn't difficult to guess. A brown-skinned girl in these parts either had parents who'd escaped slavery or had done so herself.

"Heard tell there were slave-catchers coming in from the coast," Sol continued. "Miz Marshall thought it a fine plan to bring the girls over here and Irene among them, for all the world like they was going on a picnic, as long as Irene was out of the Nag's Head before the Regulators set in."

I shuddered at the thought of such men sitting in the main room of the inn, eating my parents' food and scraping through the trappers and townsfolk for any word of a runaway girl.

"She couldn't have gone to Haasi Town?" I murmured, thinking of the Maroon settlement and wishing Irene could've stayed. The girls would miss her, especially Meg. They were the youngest two, always gossiping and giggling, and sometimes when I'd gone into the girls' rooms of a morning to bring in coffee, Meg was curled up in Irene's bed.

"Haasi Town is empty tonight," Sol said. "The Maroons have scattered in case the slave-catchers try to burn them out."

Those marsh lights I'd seen from the wagon danced behind my eyes. If the Maroon people were hidden in boltholes across the Glades, who else might be abroad? Ada Nuit was the Maroons' queen. A shiver ran through me again as I imagined the Corpse Lady and her shades brought to bear on Regulators. If she'd led Jonnie and the runaways to Haasi Town, it wasn't hard to imagine her leading slave-catchers straight into quicksand.

"God damn them all." Jonnie sounded as though she was choking. "Thank you for helping her, Sol."

He shrugged. Light caught his knife. He was whittling at something, cool as you pleased. "Now Miss Jonnie, would you like to see a thing? It might take your mind off Regulators and such." He inclined his head toward me, hat brim shading his eyes. "Miss Bess, I don't like to show you this, but since you're here, I suppose there's no help for it."

I snorted. "Why, Solomon Rowland, if you think I'm just going to stay behind like a maiden auntie whilst you spirit my girl away to God-knows-what…" I made my voice lighthearted for Jonnie's sake. It was the eternal joke about Sol, how popular he was with ladies, and maybe it would make her giggle now. "This certainly is a night for secrets."

"This is one Jonnie will do well to pass on to certain of our acquaintances," Sol said. He patted Buck's nose again. "Tie up the horses. They'll not like where we're headed."

I didn't like where we were headed, once we arrived.

At the back of the barracks there was a corral and a long barn, full of the usual sounds of horses at night. There was also a pen, shabbily constructed of rough pine slats that stood taller than a man's height, and inside the pen were limerunners. There were too many of them for the space, I knew that at a glance, and they weren't being fed properly—that was obvious by the way they snapped at one another, by the gashes on flanks and noses, by the white-eyed looks they shot our way when Sol stopped a safe distance between us and the fence.

They appeared wiry, whippy even for their snake necks and hairless tails. Starved, thirsting—it came to me, a vision of the stable my pa and Jonnie had built. The strange knowledge they'd gleaned from watching, catching, learning the beasts. Among the Rebs, that knowledge would be greater than gold.

Jonnie's hand found mine and clenched it tight. I wanted to turn her face into my shoulder, or carry her back to the wagon and chivvy the horses until they bolted for home. If I found the sight distasteful, I knew it dug into her like a knife beneath the ribs.

"They've begun buying up any that were already in human hands." Sol's voice was barely above a whisper, his breath tickling the top of my head. "They don't know what to do with them, that's clear, but they'll figure it out."

When they did, the Confederacy would have a force of fighting horses, deadlier than warmbloods with their hooves and poundage. The Rebels would torment the limeys, drive them nastier than they were born to draw out their killing instincts. The water horses would be nothing but walking weapons, to be unleashed with as much brutality as possible and abandoned to a battlefield death when their purpose was spent.

Jonnie's breath ran shallow, ragged. My fingers turned numb from her grip on them, but I didn't shake her away. We were tucked to the side of the pen, half behind the barn, and as we watched, two men appeared and went into a fenced-off slot between the gate and the roiling mass of limeys. One was black, with gaunt cheekbones and a lean frame that spoke of starvation. The other was the stout white man who'd come to the Nag's Head and baited Jonnie with his questions.

"That one there." The commander's voice carried across the pen. He pointed to a gray, taller and bulkier than most limeys I'd seen. "Rope him in."

Even at a distance, in the spotty torchlight, the slave man's face was written over with resignation. He uncoiled a whip in one hand and a length of rope in the other. He was good with the lariat; it took a single toss to get the rope over the gray's neck. Muscle corded down the man's arms when the limey thrashed. The water horse's fellows swarmed closer, sensing weakness, and the man's whip snapped out. The crack of it scattered them, though I knew it wouldn't take long for them to come snaking back.

The gray squalled, his forelegs stiff and plowing into the dirt against the man's efforts to drag him into the smaller pen.

"I can't," Jonnie whispered. The thickness of her voice told me she was swallowing tears. "Sol, please. Please let's go, I can't stand here and watch this."

If she watched them any longer, she'd leap over the fence and try to turn them loose, or throttle the Rebel with his own kerchief, and get herself eaten alive or shot. I couldn't bring a body back to Maria. I hated the sight of them too, all cooped together and Lord knew what the Confederates were doing to them—trying to ride them, teaching them to savage men or warmblood horses—but every second we stood here was a second closer to Jonnie abandoning all sense.

"Only look at them," I whispered, my lips close to her ear. "The Rebs don't know how to keep 'em right, like you do." My throat was dry but I kept talking, clamping my thumb over hers. "They're too far from water, they're sure not turning 'em out. It won't work, don't you think? It can't."

Jonnie's fingers flexed against mine. I prayed my words were distracting her, catching her mind back. Maybe it was true and maybe it wasn't, but either way, we couldn't fix this tonight.

After a moment Sol moved next to me. The warmth of him was stifling in the summer night as he bent down. "Put this in your next missive, Miss Bess." His hand landed on Jonnie's shoulder, large and firm, turning her when she made a move toward the pen. "You'll have to be alive to ride that message east, Miss Jonnie."

She said nothing back to him, and nothing to Miz Marshall when the girls came back out to the wagon past midnight, and not even anything to me on the drive home—but at least Sol's words had struck true.

She needed to be alive.

CHAPTER EIGHT

"*Y*OU CAN'T SEW ANY faster?"

"If I sew any faster, the fabric will catch fire." My voice was a touch testy. I was whipping stitches into the velvet jacket as quickly as I knew how, and Jonnie was just pacing, her boots wearing holes through the floorboards. "It's not only a matter of sewing, and you know it. The symbols have to be right, otherwise the intelligence men won't be able to read them, and—"

"Why do we need the symbols at all? I know what I need to tell them."

That stopped my needle entirely. I jabbed it through the sleeve, where a tiny horse was taking shape along the cuff, and looked at Jonnie. "You aren't supposed to know any of the messages."

She scoffed. "Bess, I can't hardly avoid knowing this one, can I? I saw it with my own eyes!"

"Yes, but the Northerners mustn't know that." Had she forgotten how this worked? "They'll say you're— compromised if they find out."

It was some complicated business set up by the North's agents, its wheels greased by Sol Rowland who knew everyone, but as far as I could tell, their general mode seemed to be that the fewer people who knew a thing, the better… and the messenger was never supposed to be able to recite back a message. It was one thing for me to know a piece of information, safe in the Nag's Head, sewing my curtains and braiding my hair and leaning over the bar just a touch too far to give the customers a glance down my bodice. Nobody figured there were many thoughts in my head beyond the inn and Jonnie and the latest in petticoats. Sol had chuckled to Ma and Pa about what a good trick it was, the details in my head and their outlines on Jonnie's back.

The Union men preferred as many middlemen as possible—to disperse blame, perhaps, or keep any one person from having all the pieces of the puzzle.

"All I know's I'd be halfway to Fort Leon by now," Jonnie muttered. "They got to know the Rebs already have a dozen limeys. How'd they rustle up so many, so fast? I wish we'd been able to see how they're training 'em. I wish…" Her jaw worked, teeth clenching beneath her tawny-smooth skin. "Lord, Bess, why'd I have to be so weak?"

"You're not weak." My voice was faraway now, drifting as it did when the stitches I was making in cloth wrapped through my mind and all my focus went into the thread. "You love them."

She loved them, and maybe I should've been jealous as some girls were jealous when their young men went around with other girls, but Jonnie's love was big enough for our whole world. For Maria and my parents, for the plain old horses that drew our plow and wagon, for me and the Sanctus River and the limerunners she coaxed out of the water, for her father whom he'd never met but whose face glowed in our minds on the strength of Maria's tales.

I doubted she had much love for the Union, seeing as the United States of nearly two decades before had been just fine enslaving her parents. But the Confederacy was an evil thing, no bones about it; Maria had drilled into all of us the necessity of fighting that snake wherever it reared its head, before it'd had a fancy name to call itself.

I thought again of Haasi Town and the Maroon women who'd taught Maria to swim and me to braid round grass rugs, of the children born to African people and Creeks and Seminoles, their parents hunted and them born free. Once before the Maroon settlement in the marshes had been burned out, when Jonnie and I were twelve or so, and the kitchen of the Nag's Head had become a hospital.

It was a slippery thing, this place of ours. Somehow I'd never noticed just how uneasy the peace was, until the Rebs had come along and dashed it utterly.

"I got some plan to go over there and slip the gate on that pen," Jonnie said. "Wouldn't take more than that. They must know how dangerous it is, keeping the beasts cooped together."

Maybe they did, and maybe they didn't. Maybe the people they'd bought the limeys off of hadn't bothered to pass along any useful knowledge, only counted their coins and washed their hands of blood. Maybe the stories folk had told them of limeys were too far-fetched to credit, and maybe Sawgrass had suddenly grown tight-lipped, for even if we couldn't always agree about runaways or trappers, we were agreed on outsiders.

I tied off the little embroidered horse and began stitching a row of whorls on either side of him. They were decorative, no hidden message, but the tight-curled shape was a place to store protection.

Jonnie stopped her paces and went to the window. She sat down on the wooden seat and drew her legs up, her profile solemn and sharp against the moonlight outside. She was right that I needed to work faster; the sky was beginning to lighten toward the gray of dawn. We'd driven back with Miz Marshall and the girls well past midnight, and I wasn't sure the coins clinking in my apron pocket were worth the fear that the garrison had planted inside me.

"I know how I'd do it," Jonnie said, her voice low.

I was afraid she meant she knew how she'd get back to the garrison and raise hell. "Do what?"

"If—" I heard her swallow. I wanted to sing, drive away her pain for a time with something silly—one of Rafael Suarez's filthy chanties, maybe—but I was tired and the sewing took all my attention. "If I had a limey to train like that, why, it wouldn't take much. I'm afraid they'll manage it, Bess, I'm so afraid."

It was strange to hear her say that. She was a daredevil, riding her races and training her water horses, noosing gators with Aaron and the other boys, playing mumble-de-peg with trappers by the inn's fireplace. She hadn't been afraid, not a lick, when she'd downed the Sanctus bridge and held up a Rebel gun-cart and left two men in the sand. But in the lamplight, I saw her face turning pale and paler, as though she was ill, and her eyes huge as ink-blots on paper.

"People say they're evil," she said. "Limeys, they ain't evil, there's no evil creature in the world but men. They got a better nature, but Bess, it's so easy to let them slip the other way. To encourage them." She hid her face in her hands, and her words came out muffled. "Now and then somebody asks for a fighting limey. Your pa doesn't like it, but even if he did, I wouldn't do it. Now that's evil. Making 'em savage like that."

So that was Jonnie's definition of evil. She'd never been much for church, although she prayed to Maria's God and Ma's and the Maroons'. I smoothed the red jacket's left sleeve and flipped it over, checking my symbol-patterns and the decorations alike, studying each seam in lapels and hem for loose stitches and gapping. There were little nothings Maria knew of but wouldn't tell me about, braids and knots and patterns that tore things apart instead of keeping them together, or cast nets over people. *Shackles*, Maria called such work, and I was never to do them, never to look for them, never to turn my hand thus.

"I don't know," I said primly. "I'm not convinced. You could see it—they don't know what they're about. Those limeys were bone-dry, all listless, just about ready to eat each other up. You always say turning 'em out is half the taming. Letting them have their head a bit. Even with that poor slave man to help, the Rebs won't manage it."

It. It rose in my mind, a vision of what the Confederacy wanted: a shoreline of battle dressed in Union blood where sailors had been met by something out of nightmare, dripping from the long dog-teeth of the water horses. I might be right about how the Rebs were going about training their limeys, and Jonnie might be wrong about the inevitability of their cruelty. But suddenly I feared more than anything that what the Rebs couldn't have, they'd merely destroy.

"I do believe you listen to me sometimes, Bess." Jonnie's lips twitched upward a touch. "Don't go telling my secrets to those soldiers in the dining room tomorrow."

I wanted sorely to drape the jacket over her bare shoulders, admire its red depth against her skin. I wanted to hold her close, so tightly and sweetly she'd stay.

"I hate the notion of that stout man learning what he needs to," Jonnie concluded. "If I could take that out of my head, I would. These past nights, all I seen when I close my eyes is that man hurting limeys." She gazed over at me, black brows furrowed together. "And now I don't need to imagine it. That's what he's doing."

I pressed my lips to the jacket lapel, where I'd sewn the most important symbols for the Northerners. It was a seal like wax dripped onto letters, a last mark that I had to believe kept Jonnie safe. Shaking out the jacket, I smiled at her, though the expression tore at my heart.

"You'll have to help stop him, then."

Had our parents caught wind of our evening's activities, Pa would've found a year's worth of odds and ends to keep Jonnie working around the inn and off Keke's back. She wasn't supposed to ride messages during daylight hours, with that velvet coat like a flag for all the countryside to see. But she'd donned it and was racing down the highway toward Fort Leon before dawn had cracked the horizon, and so it was me standing in the kitchen to get the rough side of Ma's tongue.

"What were you thinking, Elizabeth? Letting her charge off at this hour? She won't be at the coast 'til nigh on noon." Ma's fingers pinched at my chin, forcing me to look at her. "It ain't safe for her to be out there with those—those spies in the middle of the blasted day."

"You're so worried about her," I said right back, because if I didn't sass Ma I was going to cry. "Worried about Jonnie? Three guns on her and that hellbeast beneath her?" As though I wasn't worried to a frazzle myself. "Not worried enough to keep her inside when she goes off to hold up Reb shipments and let Keke bleed men dry." Ma made a startled noise, and Maria's lips drew together in a hard line, but I kept going. "For certain you're not worried enough to stop her going right into the middle of the garrison and seeing things she oughtn't to, things that'll drive her mad if she can't stop 'em."

"That woman," Ma said, and released my face. She jammed a spoon into her cornbread batter, stirring furiously. She meant Miz Marshall, I realized. "I should never have let you two go with her. For all the good it did—"

She reached for me again, palm smudged with meal and brushing one of my braids. I twitched away.

"Don't seem like you're worried about me at all, Ma." Hurt sparked in her eyes. "Oh, for certain, Bess! Go work your little nothings on those girls, make them pretty but not too pretty, keep them safe but not so safe they can't conduct their business. Go ride over to a nest of soldiers and traitors and see just what evil they're up to." Ma's hand fell back to her side. Her fingers twisted her apron. "Put it all right in front of Jonnie, who'll never be able to resist it, and then it'll be your fault when she's not safe."

We stared at one another, the small morning noises of the kitchen surrounding us. I wanted to let the kettle's scream and the twist-and-pop of fatty bacon on the hearth comfort me—wanted Ma to hug me close, wanted to sink into the scent of coffee and watch Maria make gingerbread and pretend all I had to do was serve the men in the main room, smile and flirt, keep tea and hominy coming until Jonnie's chores were done and we could sneak off to the cypresses beyond the barn.

Maria laughed suddenly. "I do believe we raised you two right, Bess." She left off turning the bacon and sat down on a stool near the fireplace, patting her apron like I was still small enough to sit on her lap. "Oh, I wish you could've met my John. There's more of him in you than seems possible." Her eyes burned into me, searching every point of my face like somehow Jonnie's father would gaze back at her. "His sweetness and fire. Like the honey and the bee. And Jonnie has his spirit."

A sob pushed out of my throat despite my attempts to shove it back down.

"Jonnie will do what she will," Maria said gently. "Well she might, with you to defend her. Now take these out to the men." She lifted me a tray of turnovers, their plump tops glazed with egg and crackling-warm. My belly rumbled. "Tuck one in for yourself, first."

"Maria," I said, my voice small and broken. She only nodded. I ate a turnover as quick as I could without scalding my tongue—it was squirrel and greens inside the dough—and then fled into the dining room, not giving Ma another look.

"Where's your girl, Bess?" called Jamie Little when I stopped near his table with the coffee pot. He grinned up at me through his beard, one paw wrapped around his cup and the other around Marta's hip. "Heard tell of a fox-hunt on the Leon road this morning. Men and dogs running down a crimson coat. What do you say?"

"I say your ears are bigger than other parts, from the sound of it," I snapped. I was in no mood to be pleasant to Jamie Little. Slopping coffee into his mug, I beamed at Marta on his knee. "That about right, Miss Marta?"

Marta giggled, then smoothed her hands over her smile as Jamie snarled. "Mouth like that gets girls in trouble."

"I was born into trouble, Jamie Little." I made to move past him, the pot clenched in my hands. "Born and raised in the trouble of serving breakfast and smiles to men like you."

He threw his cup aside, splattering coffee across the table, and grabbed me. "Now, Bess, don't be cross. If it's true about Jonnie Bruner, why, I'll take care of you, never you fear."

I shoved against him with enough force to send Marta scattering. "Don't you touch me, and don't dare lay your filthy mouth on Jonnie. Don't come near her name with your curses." He leaned back in his chair, surprise filtering into the leer on his face. "You speak of her again and I'll set a mark on you such as you carry it all your days."

The grayish tinge to his Irish-pasty face was satisfying. He was buccaneer-born, was Jamie Little, and sea raiders had a story of the black spot, which could be given to a man at any time and never taken away until he was dead of it.

"Do you think I can't?" I said, and all the while I was still beaming, my best innkeeper's smile across my face. I looked pretty this morning, because once Jonnie was gone there was no possibility of sleeping and so I'd spent my hours until daybreak washing my hair and carefully braiding it again; I looked lovely and soft and fit only for the domestic sphere, and I wanted Jamie to fear me. "Do you think I won't tie up your manhood in sawgrass and barbed wire? That I won't bundle away your performance in a birdcage? I could sell your very soul to Ada Nuit herself and would you even notice it gone?" It was hot in the main room, I thought, and on its heels came the realization that my voice had gone all singsong, high-pitched in a keen. "Best believe I'll stitch your likeness into my embroidery hoop and—snip!"

I snapped my fingers, and Jamie jerked in his chair. He muttered something, hoarse and low. Marta had retreated to the bar, where she and Meg watched me with huge eyes. Around the room men had gone quiet over their coffee and checkers.

"Miss Bess," someone said, and a hand looped around my wrist. Sol Rowland peered down at me, his mild brown eyes concerned. "Let me fetch you some water."

"You," I said, anger flaring brighter inside my breast. "Why, I've words for you too, just let me—"

"Bess." He propelled me past the bar and my father, who'd just come in from the back door, sending Pa a friendly nod. The kitchen door banged open and Sol released my arm. "Jamie's not wrong about your mouth, though his reasoning may not be sound."

"I won't hear it from you!" I told him, though my head spun and heat surged in my temples, a pounding headache. I remembered vaguely that I'd had nought to eat this morning but Maria's turnover. "How could you, Sol? How could you show her that last night?"

"Sit down before you fall down," Sol said. Out of the corner of my eye I saw Maria turn from the stove. My mother was nowhere to be seen. I felt the back of a chair at my knees and tried to arrange myself on it with some dignity. Sol shook his head. "If Jonnie's in the business of intelligence, well, don't you suppose it would benefit those Northerners to have all the facts at hand?"

"You could've just told her." Strands of hair stuck to my throat, sweaty and clinging, though I had no notion of how they'd escaped from my braids. "By God, you didn't have to haul her over there to see with her own eyes."

Sol studied me. He was still standing, towering over me, his usual easy smile nowhere in sight. He'd found time to change, I noted with some disgust, between taunting Jonnie with terrible facts and berating me in my own house: his checked vest was gone, swapped for a natty linen waistcoat and striped trousers. He never looked like a trapper, Sol, never wore deerhide or fox furs, always appeared washed and combed and handsome.

"She took it so hard?" he said at last, and I laughed in disbelief.

"What do you suppose? She dragged me home and begged me to sew what we saw into that coat so's she could ride it to Fort Leon straightaway. And now Jamie Little says men are after her—whose fault is that, Solomon Rowland?"

Maria's hands settled onto my shoulders, and a cool wet cloth pressed my forehead. I leaned back, sighing at the comfort of her form, her flour-and-oil scent.

"She'll do well to temper those feelings some," Sol said. An odd expression crossed his face, befuddlement or reflection. "'Tis a strange market just now, Bess."

"Market?"

"A lot of currents flowing, and not all of them in harmony. Jonnie might could use a little restraint in swimming those currents." Long fingers tapped the elbow they cupped, tugging Sol's still-crisp sleeve. "Be a bit more like your friend Miz Constantia Marshall. Never hurts to play smart odds. Diversify your business."

I stared at him, trying to ferret out his meaning. What was Miz Marshall's business, after all? Surely she didn't have the means to broker such a deal for limerunners as the Rebels had managed to catch. She'd sent Irene on to safety, well away from slave-catchers. Surely she wouldn't then turn around and sell out all our safety for whatever pittance the Rebs mustered.

"Why, you're not on their side?"

He laughed. "A trapper's on no one's side, as well you know." Surveying me, he reached out to tuck a lock of hair behind my ear. "As much information as I have, the better business runs. War's no time for sentimentality. She'll get herself killed over those creatures and you know it."

He wasn't wrong, but it was heartless to say. Heartless to think he could show her proof of the Confederacy's plans, their torment of the limeys in pursuit of a dangerous fighting force, and Jonnie would take it on the chin. Heartless to believe she could see them as he did, flesh waiting to be converted to money.

"It'd be a waste," Sol said, low beneath the clatter of spoon and skillet as Maria returned to the stove. "Save her from herself, Bess."

Save her. Defend her. It sounded so much crueler outside my own head, like not Sol and not Maria and not even me truly knew her.

I put my head down on the table and cried, and neither Maria nor Sol tried to stop me.

CHAPTER NINE

$\mathcal{M}$A SENT ME TO town with charity baskets for the church, which I supposed she thought would calm my nerves some—which it did, for the time it took me to get there. Away from the Nag's Head, outside in the daylight and the breeze, I remembered that the world around us was turning… that there were horses who weren't limeys and folk who just rode them or hitched them to ploughs, that some people made honest trades at barrel-making and teaching little ones, that Sawgrass was bigger than me and Jonnie and the inn.

It was a pretty day, the sun high in a soft blue sky. My braids were a sweltering sweaty mass on the back of my neck by the time I got to the town proper. Sawgrass didn't unfurl as Sawyer did, fifteen miles northeast, being situated where the prairie started to rise. Sawyer's buildings were visible from a distance, a few miles out, so that you knew to expect the town before you were in it. They were arranged all neat and sharp, a grid of church and school and tall storefronts around the central square. Somebody had planned that, a few mayors back, and it all made sense.

Sawgrass, now: Sawgrass rose up from the marshes and cypress jungle ringing Okeechobee like a bird popping out of the clock my great-grandmother Sarah had brought over from Germany. It was a sprawl among the water oaks and bay laurels, because it'd been built over the years instead of all at once, a rag doll well-loved by all the girls in a family instead of a paper doll snapped out of a sheet of pasteboard with crisp edges.

The Spanish church, right down by the river's edge, was the oldest building in town, stone and tile and strange language chanted at dawn and dusk.

The ferry and docks had come next, out of necessity, and by now none of their boards were original.

Haasi Town, the Maroon settlement, had appeared overnight, or so the story went—raised up from whole cloth by Ada Nuit's own hand to shelter her runaways. Maria said it was likelier the settlement had always been there in one form or another, and white men were just slow to notice things that didn't concern them.

The farrier and smith, the general store, the schoolhouse, the Lutheran church, the scrawl of cabins and homesteads spiraling out through the scrub, even the little prison… all of that was Sawgrass, and all of it mine. Walking into the town's heart with a basket of food weighting either arm felt like stepping into an embrace. Maybe my family was no good at comforting me today, but town might do the trick.

I hefted my right arm and its burden to tuck strands of hair back into their braids and smiled at Miss Anthorpe where she stood smoking a long black cigarillo on the schoolhouse porch. My cheeks needed no pinching for color, not when they'd already gone rosy from the heat. I'd run upstairs after Ma had told me to go visit the Lutherans and stop moping, and changed my dress for one that hadn't had Jamie Little and Sol Rowland's paws all over it, and I felt—

Better, if not good. Jonnie and Keke lingered in the back of my mind like phantoms, like swamp-fire rising to line the corpse roads at night. When I murmured a prayer for them, it wasn't to God above but to Herself, Ada Nuit, and my own soul be damned.

"Well, Miss Elizabeth!" said Warren Almquist the elder when I popped my head through the door of the little room at the back of the Lutheran church that served as the reverend's study. "How nice to see you outside the inn for a jaunt."

The reverend himself blinked at me from behind his desk. "Bess, it's sure good of Maria and your ma to send those along. If you'd like to leave them in the icehouse, the ladies are due in for the noon dinner line shortly."

"The ladies" were a gaggle of do-gooder wives and spinsters who tallied up donated items and lugged along their own offerings each afternoon to do for a few families in the area. Some had too many mouths to feed, some had a man who could no longer work for love of drink or ailment, and some just liked Maria's molasses loaves but considered themselves too Christian to come eat them at the Nag's Head with the trappers and working girls.

I curtsied to Reverend Haylock. "Yessir. I'm to tell you my pa has a side of venison for your supper tonight if you'd care to join us. He's in Sawyer on business, but he'll be home for supper, sure as the sun sets."

I sent another prayer up that Jonnie would be home for supper too, this one to the man of the house. I doubted that God paid much attention to one such as me, but maybe things went better if the prayer came from one of his own churches.

"Your pa's a godly man," the reverend said, and sniffled. He was a weedy Ohioan who hadn't yet cottoned to the exuberance of flowering plants in our part of the countryside. His nose ran like a well-pump regardless of season. "That's kindly. Send my regards and my happy acceptance, if you will."

I wouldn't have exactly called Pa "godly," seeing as he hadn't darkened a church's doorstep since my christening. He'd tussled it out something nasty with the previous Lutheran clergy over withholding food and supplies from Haasi Town after the inhabitants built their own church and kicked out the Lutheran missionary. He got on well enough with Reverend Haylock, probably because Reverend Haylock left the Maroon people alone and didn't try to put the fear of God into Pa over the dinner table.

"If you see my son out there," Almquist said, "send him along. We've some business to square away with the good reverend." He beamed at Reverend Haylock and rapped on his desk. The reverend, if anything, looked even sicklier. "I'll say, Miss Elizabeth, I pray I see Warren with a nice young lady like you soon enough."

My stomach roiled at the thought of Warren the younger bothering any girl, nice or not. I nodded and smiled again at the two of them, and scampered as quickly as possible out the back door.

The icehouse was blessedly cool and dark, creeping on as we were to noon. I unpacked the baskets, removing the molasses cakes from their cloths and stacking them beside cold sliced venison wrapped in fronds. There was a jug of gooseberry jelly and one of honey from Pa's hives, and corn-cakes on which they could be slathered. I patted each bit, proud of how generous Maria and my parents were, and arranged everything neatly on the shelves. As I was folding the empty clothes and net sack into my baskets, someone opened the icehouse door. I turned, expecting one of the do-gooder ladies, and saw Warren Almquist the younger.

"Well! There you are, wherever you've been—your pa's in the church waiting on you."

"That what he said?" Warren replied, lounging against the threshold like he wasn't letting all the cold out. "I can think of one or two things I'd rather be doing than cozening the preacher."

Some of the icehouse chill ran into my bones. "I don't see what reason you'd have to talk to the preacher about anything, let alone something crooked."

"At any rate," Warren went on like I hadn't even spoken, "this business concerns you all at the Nag's Head." He came further into the icehouse, stepping close to me and smiling down, one hand drifting to rest on my shoulder. "So far as I can see, I'll be ahead of schedule, do I get you back to the inn by noon."

"Let me go if you know what's healthy." I jerked my arm away, but his fingers dug in, so hard my flesh stood out pale between them and the neckline of my dress. "Warren Almquist, I swear to Christ I'll scream in a minute."

"No need for that, Bess," he said. He smiled still, blond hair stuck to his forehead in sweaty clumps and blue eyes mild. "You're going to the Nag's Head and so am I. It's a mighty hot day and it'd be a sore sight, you fainting on the road with this sun. Don't you think it makes sense, letting me drive you home?"

I didn't want to let him do anything. I hadn't wanted to let him see under my skirts, when I'd been young and still had to go to the schoolhouse every other day and the boys chased me and Jonnie and the other girls. I hadn't wanted him anywhere close to me or the limeys, that morning just a few days before, and I didn't want him in the icehouse now, and I certainly didn't want to climb up on his wagon and make cheery conversation while he drove, too slow, toward my family.

But his hand on my shoulder clamped like a vise, his fingers splayed across my collarbone in a way that hurt more than I figured it should. I figured too that it was better to be on his wagon-seat in broad daylight, for all the town to see, instead of in the chilly dark of the icehouse, where anything might happen with no one to witness.

So I smiled too and let him tuck my hand beneath his arm, and we went out to the wagon and horse waiting in front of the church.

It was usual to see folk coming and going from the inn's front door and barn at all hours. But as Warren's wagon rolled up our front drive, I saw not a flicker of movement in the yard—not even Rex dozing beneath his favorite cabbage palm. No trappers walked the shell path to the door, and no townsfolk were hitching up at the posts; the only people in sight, other than Warren beside me on the seat, were two men on either side of the inn's door.

My heart kicked up inside my chest at the sight of them: gray uniforms, sweat-stained, caps tugged low to shade their eyes and rifles slung loose over shoulders.

It was too quiet around these parts. You could often hear the main room's ruckus before you set foot inside, and the silence rang in my ears.

"Rex!" I called when Warren drew up his horse, and clapped, praying for the old hound to come trotting out from the bushes. "Here, boy!"

"I'd not look for him," Warren said, all casual like he knew the habits of my dog.

"Well, he'll be wanting a bone to gnaw," I returned, trying to keep a wobble from my voice. "He knows it's noon meal just as well as any of us."

Warren rubbed his stomach with one hand and tipped up his straw hat with the other. His eyes swept over the inn. "I'll be looking forward to some of Maria's sweet corn-pone, for certain. Won't you show me inside, Miss Bess?"

"Why, you know the way as well as I do," I said. He hopped down from the wagon and held out a hand, which I ignored in favor of dropping down to the sand myself. "I need to see whether Pa's back from Sawyer."

"He ain't back."

"Aren't you Mister Know-It-All today?" I snapped. "I believe I'll see for myself whether he's in the barn, Warren Alm—"

He grasped my elbow with a wrench, turning me toward the front door and the Rebel men there. "Your pa ain't here, Bess. Now come on."

Let no one say I've ever made things easy for a man. I twisted my arm in his grip until the skin was red and sore, and shoved at him with the other hand, dug my heels into the walkway and kept up a stream of hollering, but it made no use. He was taller than me and twice as heavy, and I didn't at all like the expression on his face as he pushed me along, half grimace and half leer. The two soldiers at the door nodded to him and barely looked at me, for which I supposed I ought to be grateful.

The interior of the inn, which I knew by heart, gave no comfort. There were more soldiers in gray in the front hall, the gun-racks on either wall bristling with rifles and shotguns and pistols. I loathed the sight of our big bearskin rug beneath their boots. But it was the main room that sent chills down my arms when we walked through—for it looked normal, nearly: trappers at their cards and dice, girls draped over their shoulders and knees. Yet it was silent, the usual laughter and arguing and occasional fists nowhere in sight, and every face was tense, from Anne Sloakum's china-white complexion and pointed chin to Jamie Little's ginger beard.

I counted off the men. Another six or so men from the garrison, whose names I didn't know and didn't care to know. Jamie, Ward Henteeth but not his sister, a half-Seminole cowman called Levi Cypress. Rafael Suarez was nowhere to be seen, nor Solomon Rowland. A few townsmen sat among the trappers, Miss Anthorpe's father and Martin Healy the ferryman and—my heart leapt up into my throat—Reverend Haylock with Warren Almquist the senior.

"What's going on?" I reached out for Marta as I passed her by the bar, but she flinched away. "Where's my mother?"

"The kitchen, Miss Bess," said Warren. "Maria too. They keep quiet and all will be well, you hear?"

Anne shook her head slowly, silently, when I tried to make for the kitchen door. Warren grabbed my other arm and twisted both behind my back. "None of that, sweetling. Upstairs you go."

Upstairs. As my feet hit the bottom step, I tried to fit the pieces together. Pa still in Sawyer, so it seemed, and maybe Warren knew that for sure because someone was keeping Pa away from the Nag's Head. Ma and Maria in the kitchen, and no getting to them nor they to me… if they were truly there. Aaron, our horse-boy, who knew? I hoped he and Rex were hunting, or out on Okeechobee with the Maroons, somewhere safer than here. Jonnie at Fort Leon or maybe—

I pushed that thought away.

"So what is all this?" I said to Warren, craning my neck to peer at him behind me on the stairs. "Turned traitor and your new friends decided they wanted to camp somewhere a sight nicer than the garrison? If only they'd asked, I'm sure we had room."

My parents wouldn't have rented any of the rooms to Confederacy rabble. Or would they have? The inn was neutral, but how far did that extend? There were tales of my great-grandmother turning blind eyes to British soldiers who'd sailed into Fort Leon during the War for Independence. I thought of Pa feuding with the old Lutheran reverend when I was barely out of Ma's womb.

Maria would never have allowed it, Confederate men inside the Nag's Head.

Warren laughed. "Traitor, is it? Such fine ideals from a jumped-up slut." He pressed me close to the garret hallway's wall, my cheek against the whitewashed boards. "The Union will fall, Bess. Only natural that rotten things should collapse and strong things rise." His breath smelled as though he'd raided Miss Anthorpe's still. "Unnatural is what you are. You and Jonnie."

A voice sounded from my bedroom door. "Get her in here and then leave her alone, for God's sake."

Solomon Rowland was frowning when Warren pushed me through the door. He let me loose a mite too soon and I used the advantage to fly at Sol. "And you too? You bastard, Sol—whatever this is, I swear I'll—"

"Don't." His voice was flat and his eyes too, not a speck of light in their warm brown, and I saw that he wasn't alone. My heart crumpled at the sight of gray uniforms in my room, Jonnie's room, our sanctuary. "Bess, it's best if you calm yourself."

"Don't throw your back out of joint being too kind," I flared. "Take your gentle words to the outhouse where they belong. If you've hurt my mother—"

"Your ma is safe."

"And Maria?"

Warren spat onto the rug, one Maria had braided when Jonnie turned twelve. All the blood drained from my face and throat, a sensation like cold springwater flowing down my body. He didn't seem to notice. He gazed at me and said, "You care so much for that Negro bitch? It's her daughter you might think of."

I laughed, a wild half-shriek boiling in my throat. "Jonnie's safe and you'd never catch her if you had a thousand years to do it."

As I said it, I knew at once it was the heart of the matter, what they were after. Jonnie, Jonnie and her skill, her prowess, her power over these creatures the Confederates craved. I had to believe it was true… that she and Keke had made it to Fort Leon and stayed there with the Union men, maybe, or were fast enough and strong enough to outrun anyone on the road—that they'd got to Haasi Town where the Maroons would take her in and hide her, that she had Ada Nuit's hand set on her in truth, to guide her limey's demon hooves.

If she wasn't here and these men were, perhaps it was true. Perhaps she was still safe.

"Don't need a thousand years," one of the Confederates said. He stared at me too and I realized it was the man with the eyes, as Jonnie called him, the officer so bent on twisting limeys into the shape he wanted. "All we need is you, Miss Elizabeth."

My vision clouded, all my sight dissolving into white sparks and fog. Heat expanded inside my skull until I thought my head would burst. I spoke before I could think about it, my words seeming very far away. "I don't know who you've been talking to, mister. She loves those water horses more than she could ever love me."

For a moment I hoped that was true, this thing I'd never believed before, if it meant she'd stay far away from the Nag's Head. I would have given her up over and over, if that was what ensured her life. With all my heart I urged her to follow Ada Nuit's troop into mist and nothingness, if that kept her safe.

"I think not," the Confederate officer said. "She'll come home, if only to secure your safety."

"She won't," I said, and my voice ran away with me. "She'll catch wind, because there's a fair few faces missing downstairs—oh, Sol, you know who I mean, don't you? You know there's more than one of your fellows who aren't turncoats, who'll tell her the moment they see her? She'll hear what's afoot and she'll stay away and you'll never get your filthy goddamned fighting limeys, you—"

Save her from herself, Sol had told me. Tried to warn me, with whatever scrap of decency he'd had left, thought to remind me of her high ideals, her fierce belief, her love.

Warren's hand covered my mouth and his arm crossed my chest, jerking me against him. He held me while I thrashed, until I bit him. Then he thrust me away, hard enough to send me stumbling into Jonnie's oak chest. I clipped my knee on its corner and toppled, the pine boards punishing beneath my palms.

The men let me stay there, a sick sort of pity written over Sol's face. The room grew silent. It was warm in the garret, past noon now and the sun outside still brutal. The heaviest of my braids dangled over my shoulder, loose tendrils clinging to damp skin. I made to push it aside, and then I thought of something.

"Sir," I said to the Reb's boots. "I apologize for my outburst. I'm just a mite distraught, my ma downstairs and all…" I looked up at him, gritting my teeth and trying a smile. "If I could just braid my hair up nice? It calms me so."

The colonel frowned. I smiled wider, though my belly quaked beneath my skirt. If only he saw me as pretty and useless, a weak girl fit for nothing but to play bait for a stronger one—if only I could get a bit of thread between my fingers, or my hair, I could try one of Maria's little nothings that might keep Jonnie safe.

"I don't think so, Bess." It was Sol, not the Reb, and before I could answer him he'd grabbed me. Lord's mercy but I was sick of men grabbing me. "Warren, your knife, if you please."

Sol was big enough to lift me off my feet entirely. He deposited me into a chair we kept by the window and the Confederate was quick with a rope. It burned my wrists, twisted through the chair's slats. Sol's hand lingered on my shoulder, where Warren had gripped me barely an hour before. There were prints on the skin. Then his fingers drifted up and laced through my hair at the base of my neck, tilting my head.

"No. Sol, please—"

"Hold her still," Warren said. "Wouldn't want to cut that pretty throat by accident."

"Sol," I whispered. His face in the mirror to our side was distant, blank. I couldn't remember how I'd thought him the best of the trappers, the most harmless—kind to Anne when he bought her services, or as kind as men could be, handsome, helping Jonnie and the Yankees with their messages. "Please don't."

"All the countryside knows," he told me. Warren's knife slashed through the largest braid at its base, and I couldn't stifle my cry. It hurt—actually hurt, far more than any cutting of hair ever could, but I felt it burn in my veins. The braid dropped to the floor. "Yes, all Sawgrass knows what you can do with these pretty locks. Better safe than choked by some witchcraft."

It seemed the most enormous betrayal: that my village and its people knew this of me, of Maria, and feared us for it, when all Maria had ever done was help.

"Haven't you ever thought," Sol said slowly, his head moving closer in the slightest weave, dizzying as a serpent. "Bess, what you could do—haven't you ever wondered what's beyond this muckland?" His beard brushed the curve of my cheek, his eyes intent but seeing past me. "What we could manage together, a witch's skills and a trapper's. It pains me, Bess, it always has. Seeing your worth tied up in these ribbons."

His offer was for me, me away from the Confederates and away from Jonnie. The contempt wreathing the words tasted as real, as bitter as vomit.

The knife-blade moved again, to each slimmer braid, five of which I'd woven into my hair this morning. With every slice the heat inside my skull grew, a black dazzle moving through my veins. It seared the space behind my eyes like a venom from a snakebite. I didn't quite know how it worked, even after all this time, but I knew whatever virtues my plaits held were diminishing, my small armor stripped from me strand by strand. Foolishly, I expected to see blood rolling down my neck. I hated the sight of myself in the mirror, my dark curls lopped off messily, chopped to my chin and higher. Ragged, ugly, where before my hair had been chief among my beauties. Long and thick, Jonnie loved to draw her fingers through it and watch me braid it. Ma envied its curls, where hers was straight. Maria trimmed it carefully once a year, and my pa had kissed the top of my head each night from the time I was small and the locks were lighter brown and baby-fine.

I'd plaited love into that hair, love and protection, and thought nothing of it. I'd thought nothing of my love for Jonnie, because it was like air—inevitable, natural, all around us—and never wondered what folk knew of it. Never tried to safeguard my heart, never realized that the trappers took note of me as I was aware of them, and here the best of them stood, using my love against me.

Against Jonnie.

The braids dropped, one by one, their power extinguished until they were nothing more than wisps on the floorboards beneath the Confederate's boots.

CHAPTER TEN

THE DAY FELL AWAY before my eyes. White-hot noon glimmered outside my window, the Lake of Spirits shining hard as glass on the horizon—but its edges grew softer as the afternoon wound on and Jonnie did not appear.

I didn't notice the passage of time at first; there were no candles lit, for the bedroom was full of sunlight and sweat gathered at the men's collars. Warren and Sol removed their jackets and loosened vests and cuffs, but the Confederate remained in his uniform, straight and sturdy and unbending.

Me, I was bent near to breaking and I knew it—I didn't doubt the men knew it—only the chair behind my back and the rope around my wrists kept me upright. The lightness of my head bothered me. I was used to the weight of hair, the thickness and width of curls and braids, the incline of my chin beneath a crown of plaits.

It drove me to distraction, the way the chopped ends swished against my skin when I moved my head. I didn't care whether the men thought me vain for glaring at my reflection in the mirror. The girl frowning back was a stranger.

Perhaps, I thought vaguely, there was no telling what any strange girl might do.

"Curse it," Warren muttered, and then his voice rose. "Hey! You down there—get to the kitchen and bring up some dinner."

There came a slow rumbling of movement down the hallway and stairwell. I wondered who in the main room would get up and retrieve food. I wondered whether Maria and Ma were safe in truth, if Warren hadn't lied to me about them being just on the other side of the door. I wondered which of the trappers were in the kitchen with them, how many soldiers; I wondered whether one of the men had hurt Ma, who had a mouth on her when she was angry or frightened, and whether they'd taken Maria's sewing basket from her, as they'd taken my hair from me.

"Now, Bess," Sol said. He bent close and pressed the sleeve of his shirt to my face. For a moment I thought he meant to smother me, but his sleeve came away with a spot of blood on it. I tasted copper on my tongue. "Don't worry that mouth so."

I worried it a bit more and then smiled at him, knowing blood smeared my teeth.

"Even with that your looks ain't spoiled," Warren said. He lifted a hank of my hair and twisted it between his fingers, tugging hard. "Even with this. Now don't you wish you'd let me help you with it, that day in your pa's barn?"

It wouldn't have made a lick of difference, in my opinion. I said nothing, giving the rope around my wrists an experimental tug. It was a good sailor's knot, one I knew but couldn't get at, and the coarse waxed rope dug into my skin. My lip wasn't the only part of me bleeding.

"Let that alone, girl," said the Reb. He didn't move from his stance at the window, but his pale eyes swept down my arms. "Try to wiggle out of there and I'll scare up a set of shackles."

I transferred my smile to him. "I'll see you in shackles on the gallows, sir."

My fingers unclenched, my wrists relaxing against their bonds. Apron tails tickled my arms, and I knew without looking that blood was smudging onto them, that I'd never get the thing clean. It was just as well; one of the ties was frayed, and the embroidered daisies along the pocket coming loose...

"What will you do?" I went on, hoping to capture the men's attention with chatter. "If Jonnie doesn't come? I suppose you'll have no more use for us here. Is it too much to ask that the Nag's Head is left to its own devices?"

"Mighty nice inn," Warren said. "Me, I'd requisition it for the Confederacy's uses." He glanced at the commander as though for affirmation, a cur-dog seeking a pat. "It's only right, in times of war."

I scoffed. "All set to join up, Warren? Why have you not already, then?" My eyelashes batted once, twice, while I rolled my apron tails together. "I'll say, it looks a mite cowardly. Like as not they won't even press you into service. Worthless whelp like you."

The flat of his hand caught my cheek and more blood flowed into my mouth. Sol cursed, disgust scrawled across his face.

The Confederate only stared at me. "Bravado will do you no good, Miss Ramsey."

"Why, I'd only like to pass the time," I said. Two lengths of thread or hair or cloth didn't form as firm a braid as three, but I'd make do. The apron tails in my hands made me feel better, stronger. I raised my voice to mask the sound of cloth tearing. "I must tell you, sir, Jonnie's never been on time in her life. Ain't that so, Warren Almquist? Late to breakfast, for she's feeding the horses, and late to supper, for she's off winning a race. I wouldn't look for her any time soon."

"They do say there's souls as would be late to their own funeral," the Confederate said. "I suppose we'll see."

That shook me some. He wasn't one to get riled up and distracted, like Warren. I had to hope he wouldn't notice my arms twitching over my makeshift braid. Even the possibility of Jonnie riding to her death hung in the air like foul smoke.

"I suppose we will. You might as well know now that she'll die before turning any limerunner to your cause."

"And a waste that'd be," the Confederate told me. He shifted on his boots, his head turned slightly from the window. The light beyond was so bright his features were blurred, indistinct. "She could be paid quite well for her stock and labor. Have a steady position within our ranks, catching and breaking the beasts. Enough coin to buy a pretty thing like you many more pretty things."

I nearly laughed. Well enough that that was what Sol and Warren thought of me—that such frivolity and falsehood were what the Confederates had learned of me. A lacquer of truth would mask any lie, was what Maria always said; if they thought Jonnie could be bought for such a price, so much the better. I pushed my giggles away and forced them into the plait taking shape between my fingers. Mirth stemming from rage was the most powerful kind, for a body that laughed in such circumstances was that much harder to break.

I didn't like to think of my body broken, or Jonnie's spirit.

"Think about it, Bess," Sol urged. His arms were folded across his chest, his lips almost smiling in their nest of beard. "You know her best. She'll come for you and all you'll do is show her reason, girl." He chuckled softly, his eyes on me seeming fond as he discussed my love. "Turn some of that wild nature toward something better."

Make Jonnie less herself.

"It's a devil's bargain," I said, my voice quiet. It was beginning to slip away, I could hear it myself, tilting dozy and faint as it did when I was embroidering or weaving and had more in my mind than just my thoughts. "I saw you that night, mister—oh, I see you remember! Well you might, with your hand still bound up. A limey'll savage you soon as look at you. You mean to send men into battle on their backs? They'll turn on you before the Yanks are even in sight."

"Bess—" Sol said again, but I hadn't stopped talking. Even though my voice was faraway, the words dropped like hail onto the floorboards.

"I was ten years old the first time I saw a man killed by a limey. Throat torn out and his belly too, shredded to bits. From across the road it looked like ribbons, silk ones, bright red and so pretty, like the ones my mother put in my hair." I'd torn the bottom of each apron string once they were twisted into a rope, then begun braiding the slender pieces back on each other. "Then three years later two limeys set on one of the ferryman's horses. A mare in heat. Did you know they turn cannibal, sir? Don't need a reason to, either. Then there was the fight at Sawyer when—ah."

I jerked my head at Warren, whose face was pale and sweaty. He looked away from my eyes, and I let my head drop and weave and jerk to keep my gaze locked to his. "You remember that, Warren Almquist. You were there." When I laughed, it sounded more like a neigh. "Oh, Sol, this was before you drifted down the river and set up in these parts. I wish to God you'd seen it! The finest backcountry entertainment, that was. You see, sir, 'twas a limey fight. You and your compatriot were right. Folk around here fight them like dogs and roosters."

I tied off the braid with the tiniest knot, teeth gritted. It was difficult going: the cloth made for shoddy material, and I couldn't see what I was doing; blood slicked my fingers and the heat had returned to my head, which by now felt dangerously loose.

"Blood ran like the Sanctus River and before long there was but one limey in the pen, still gnashing his teeth. They chew at the air when they're angry, when there's nothing more to bite. And the limey's master, why, he collected his winnings and shook hands and went in to collect his beast too." I smiled, not so much at the memory but at the skinny braid settling in between my wrists and the ropes around them. "The limey tore his arm clean off when he went to bridle it up. Worst way I ever saw a man die, sir."

I hadn't seen too many men die, thank the night and all its shades, but Sam Shoemaker lying in the sawdust with his arm three feet away really stuck out. The blood hadn't stopped, it seemed to me, even after he was gone. Face like wax and red-black still pooling, and Jonnie swore later that with each pump she could see his pulse going weak in his throat.

"And your Jonnie rides them," the Confederate said. He seemed unmoved by my story. "Rides them like angels ride clouds, so I hear. Catches them and trains them, trots that gray ghost of hers along like a pony." I hated his voice, his heavy molasses accent and every word he spoke, but they painted pictures in my head. Jonnie and Keke, two sides of a fresh-struck coin. "A no-name girl, some slave by-blow—but she rides them! Tell me, Miss Ramsey, why your Jonnie can do what no man seems able. You tell me that. Tell me why a little bit of nothing carries those beasts in her palm and you'll be downstairs with your ma before nightfall."

I didn't trust that my ma wasn't downstairs dead in her own kitchen, and so I wasn't too sure I wanted to join her just yet.

Little nothing. There was nothing little about Jonnie. She towered above me, even if she was a good sight leaner, and her name was as vast as Okeechobee. Why else would these men be here?

Little nothing. That was what Maria called her knot-work, her beautiful black plaits and her braided rugs laid smooth on the floors of newlyweds' bedrooms and atop dead folks' coffins. That was what I'd been doing this past hour and more, twining my apron threads around one another and around my bindings, braided with my own blood, and now we'd see whether it was, in truth, nothing.

I looked past the Confederate as he leaned down into my face, panting, abruptly furious. The light outside my window was still warm as honey, and the lake shone placid. But its far, dark rim shuddered as I gazed at it. It rippled and seemed to move closer. Horror and wonder mingled in my stomach as I tried to understand what I saw—whether the earth was ripping itself up in some convulsion, whether a great wave had begun on the water and was tearing inland.

Wonder drowned beneath horror as Sol moved to the window and the Reb spun to see what we were all looking at. It wasn't Okeechobee in the grip of a summer squall or an earthquake shifting the land, but horses galloping, so many that they formed a dark clot like blood spreading in water.

Jonnie was coming.

The men were crowded into the window, Warren shoving the casement open and leaning out so far I hoped he'd topple down three stories and break his fool neck.

A sound grew, one I knew well and had never thought to hear at such a pitch: hoofbeats, galloping hard, and the wet breath of a hundred throats or more, all coating the air.

In the swelling hubbub, I flexed my wrists and the ropes twined around them loosened. It was the strands that made up the rope coming apart, I knew, encouraged by the apron braid I'd tied to them… and my own blood, perhaps. Waxed to Hell or not, the rope was a binding, a marriage of fibers at its core, and I couldn't have explained it in words but I knew my little nothing was working. My skin throbbed where the ropes had cut in; I wanted to dunk my wrists in cold water and then hot and cold again, for who knew where a trapper's rope had been, but there was no time for that.

"Hold her!" the Reb bawled when I made for the door.

Arms caught me and I threw out my own arms, aiming elbows for any soft place that would take them. Sol cursed, staggering a step as my hand caught his eye, but it hadn't been a proper blow. "Goddamn you, girl—"

I shrieked, as loudly as when Aaron had stuck a large yellow grasshopper onto my ear while we were hoeing sweet potatoes, and kept yelling, scrabbling for the door. But Sol was bigger than me, stronger, and his arms pinned mine to my sides.

"Be smart, Bess," he panted, his mouth muffled in my hair. "No harm will come to you, nor her—"

I brought my knee up between his legs. "How that's for harm, Sol Rowland?"

He said something for which Ma would've sent him scurrying out the back door, but didn't let go of me. His eyes narrowed and a nasty tone came into his voice which I'd never heard before, and doubted was caused by the pain in his privates. "I said be smart. Either you keep your head and your ma and Maria stay safe, or this place burns down around your ears, all of you."

I wanted Ma and Maria safe, for certain, but he hadn't mentioned Jonnie. "Why did you help Irene escape if you were planning this all along? Is one girl so different from another?"

He laughed, to my amazement. "Jonnie Bruner is as different from Irene as noonday sun from rain." His fingers pinched the bare skin of my upper arms. "Worth her weight in gold, and what good is Irene to anyone? No skill required to sprawl on your back, Bess."

Bile rose in my throat. "You'd sell one girl into bondage as fast as you accepted coin to ferry another to freedom."

"There," the Confederate said, pointing out the window. He seemed oblivious to our conversation. He chuckled, the first sound of mirth I'd heard from him. "A rat's supposed to leave a sinking ship, not aim straight for it."

"Don't know as I'd come back for you," Warren said, sneering at me. By the look of his face, he enjoyed the sight of me kicking and straining against Sol's arms. "Too much trouble, that's you, Bess."

"Ho, there!" the Confederate shouted through the window. "Johanna Bruner!"

I whimpered, throwing myself forward. I had to at least see her before—my teeth clenched, biting back the thought. Sol let me thrash toward the window. I suppose he figured it was better than me trying for the door. Warren stepped aside, sweeping his arm out grand, as though the view was something he'd planned and delivered himself.

The yard was all horses, black coats and bay and chestnut and gray, a freak-white one here and a rosy roan there, a writhing mass like a snake pit. Despite the noon brightness, their hooves and eyes shone with an eerie moonlit glow, and perhaps it was that same bright sun nearly blinding me, but I would've sworn I saw mist or smoke rising from the dirt where they stepped. I had never wondered too hard after the origin of limeys, as Jonnie did, but now I began to believe that maybe they did spring from the waters at Hell's mouth.

Shouting erupted and I craned my neck to see who was doing it. A few men were half-visible, arms and guns waving from the front door before it slammed.

"They'll not like to go out in that," Warren said. The Reb breathed out in a long hiss. He was satisfied, practically beaming. Warren continued, "Like swimming into a nest of gators. What's your plan, sir?"

Casual as anything, the Reb placed a hand on Warren's chest and helped him right out the window.

A scream rose and then collapsed abruptly, and the commander watched, eyes unblinking and expression detached. I knew what to expect but I made myself look anyway: at the sudden swarm, the limeys diving for prey, the red spray drifting in the breeze.

"Ah," said the Reb. "Efficient little monsters."

I'd little doubt he knew that already, having penned up limeys in the garrison and set to training them. He'd seen them fight already, kill their meals and one another. Like as not he'd sacrificed a conscript or a slave man or a captured Yank to see how they killed humans.

"Johanna," the Reb called again, and I saw her at last. She sat on Keke's back in the mass of limerunners, arrow-straight, an unwavering candle flame in her red jacket. "Who shall we feed to your demons next?"

His hand latched onto my shoulder and Sol let him force me up against the window.

"Jonnie!" I cried before either of them could cork me up. Across the yard her expression was clear, dark eyes huge and mouth open in a silent shout. "Go away, damn you!"

"Let her be," she hollered back. A hand jabbed up, then balled into a fist. "Slaving trash, you let her go and I'll come talk to you."

The Confederate laughed. It echoed against my ribs, his hands clammy on my skin and his breath hot, stirring the ragged locks of my hair.

"I swear," Jonnie yelled. She and Keke began moving, the crowd of limeys parting for them like Moses and the sea. Despite the Reb at my back—despite Sol's betrayal and my own fear—awe poured through me. I didn't know where she'd rustled up so many of them, and I didn't know how she'd run so far without any of them going for Keke; I'd seen her ride and catch and train them, but never in our life together had I seen this.

Was it her, in truth? In that moment I wouldn't have sworn it was my own Jonnie, and not Ada Nuit in a girl's disguise.

They sidled right up to the house, to where Keke always came when Jonnie whistled for her at night. How many times had I watched her snaky form appear in the night like a spirit? How many times had I held my breath while Jonnie slid out the window and dropped down to meet the water horse? It had always seemed a nice little trick, but reserved for true horsewomen. I wouldn't have time to aim for the porch roof; I'd have but once to aim true.

Beneath her hat, I saw Jonnie's teeth and a thrill went up my spine. I shrieked again, no words, and beat my fists against the soldier's shoulder for effect. He had to believe I was terrified of the limeys, that I'd do or say anything to keep him from dropping me.

"Let her go," Jonnie called a third time, and I echoed her.

"Sir, please—please, if you'll just…" and my eyelashes fluttered, my lip quivered, my face nothing but pretty begging aimed toward the Confederate.

"Now then," he said, pitching his voice loud so Jonnie could hear. "Business runs a sight smoother when we all get along."

His hold on me loosened just enough. I pitched over the casement, my skirt flapping like a flag and my drawers a beacon from Sawgrass to the coast. With the sort of luck I was having today, I'd land smack among the limeys instead of on Keke's rump—

I grabbed for her tail as my legs hit bony flesh. My arm wrenched, caught in Jonnie's fingers while she hauled me up behind her. A chestnut head snapped just left of my calf, and I buried my face in Jonnie's back. The velvet jacket was soft beneath my nose. She smelled like sweat and sunshine and the astringent scent of the dye I used on thread for the coat's scarlet embroideries. They had worked, all this time; they and I had kept her safe.

Now we just had to keep her safe for a little longer.

"Bess," Jonnie said. "I swear to Christ."

"Well, it worked, didn't it?" My voice hitched, and I drew a breath. The men were pitching a fit in our bedroom, the Confederate cursing so hard I saw spittle fly from his mouth. Sol glanced down at us and then disappeared. "Now what exactly is your plan, hmm?"

She turned just enough to kiss the side of my head where curls snarled from Sol's clumsy knife. "Get to Sawyer and find our parents."

"Ma and Maria," I said. Jonnie's legs tensed along mine as she signaled Keke. "They're in the kitchen. I don't know if…"

"They're not," she said gently. "They ain't dead, Bess, and they ain't even downstairs. Miz Marshall spirited 'em away to Sawyer this morning. Warren younger opened his big mouth to Meg last night."

"But—"

Miz Marshall escorting folk to safety, while Sol made money off their flight. Lies and lies Warren had told me, Sol, all of them lying for a sole purpose—to keep me here and make Jonnie come to them.

Well, she'd come, and they wouldn't live to regret their mistake.

"Your pa, now," Jonnie continued as Keke stepped toward the front door of the Nag's Head. "He's holed up in the saloon, couple trappers there making sure he stays put. Rafael Suarez's word. Hi, Keke!"

Hooves struck the door, once and again. Keke's devilish split hooves were knife-sharp and strangely flexible, far more so than any warmblood's hoof. They tore the door to shreds as it pulsed from the other side, men shoving against it to keep us out.

"If they're all in Sawyer," I hollered to her ear, "then what in blazes are you still doing here?"

"You think I'm aiming to leave that sonofabitch alive?" she yelled back. Her ribs expanded beneath my clasping arms. "Bess, you think I'd leave the inn overrun like this? I ain't letting 'em chase me out."

She'd chase them out.

"Here." Jonnie tugged a pistol from her holster and passed it to me. "Get ready."

I didn't want to be ready. I wanted to flee back upstairs with her and find our bedroom just as we'd left it, not desecrated by horrible men.

The front door collapsed and the limerunner mass swarmed inside.

Shots and sparks lit up the hallway, but not as much as I'd expected. Men from our part of the state feared limeys more than alligators or panthers, and tonight was giving them good reason. Wet sounds of tearing and chewing flooded my ears. One or two of the beasts screamed as rifle fire hit them, but the hallway was too narrow and the water horses too many, too hungry, too fierce.

"Get out of the way!" Jonnie bellowed, and I realized we'd reached the main room. She didn't want the girls harmed. Colorful skirts flashed by. Meg, Marta, and the rest would have to bank on limeys not being able to climb stairs, though I wouldn't have placed that bet.

I bounced on Keke's back, tightening my grip around Jonnie's waist, as the limey beneath us stomped over something underfoot. My stomach rolled at the knowledge that it was almost certainly a man, and someone I knew. Hands grabbed at my leg, and I whipped the pistol down instinctively. Jamie Little fell away from us with a cry, clutching his jaw. He disappeared beneath two bay coats before I could even think to try and reach for him.

"Don't look if you don't have to," Jonnie muttered. "We just gotta… we got to get to that bastard, Bess, I don't know if they'll—"

A gun cracked, loud as Doomsday and so close I nearly believed I'd fired it myself. Keke yelped, a screech like nails dragged down Miss Anthorpe's blackboard. A figure thrashed toward us, gray jacket and cap askew, a rifle across his shoulder. I fired Jonnie's pistol, the shot wide and aimed none too well. Above the sounds of men and limeys, laughter came.

"My thanks for the display," he shouted at Jonnie. "What these beasts can do, why, it's a marvel."

He was bit, I could see, blood darkening his jacket shoulder. Still he pushed across the dining room, flailing the rifle butt at any limey that came too close. "Imagine an army such as this waiting at the Savannah coast. A tide of blood will spread north, engulfing all who come to meet it."

It was all too easy to imagine, with the evidence around us. If the Confederacy managed to grasp what it sought, Northern defenders would be trampled underfoot and chewed to shreds.

The Reb colonel grunted as a gray limey dove for him. He shot at it wildly, and an answering shriek sounded across the room. Jonnie flinched beneath my fingers. It wasn't only men hurt this evening. However she'd rounded up the water horses and chivvied them to the inn, some of them would die for it. That hurt Jonnie more than the human pain surrounding us.

"Get out, mister." Her voice was choked and hoarse. "It's already too late for your men."

Through the screams, I heard a tumult on the other side of the kitchen door. Maybe the men barricaded inside were too afraid to stay put. If we were lucky, the turncoats would be running for it by the time we got through. Sol Rowland was nowhere to be seen. I supposed it was too much to hope for that he'd caught teeth before making it to his own horse in the barn. The limeys had dispersed through the inn, bolting like Satan's armies through each room and hallway. I'd have sworn the very foundations were shaking. I wouldn't have called the Rebs cowardly for lying down in front of us and giving up the ghost.

"It's my duty to die alongside my men," the Reb gasped. He crumpled to the floor beside Keke's hooves as another horse dug its teeth into his leg. The gun tumbled from his hands. Instead of grabbing for it, he reached up, fingers straining for Keke's chest. "And an angel to bear me to Heaven."

I couldn't stand him gabbling at Jonnie, his starry-strange words and lordly manner of speaking, as though death and gore weren't swallowing us all whole. I aimed the pistol again, more carefully this time, and sank a bullet in his throat before the bay limey could start chewing that too.

"Straight to Hell on Ada Nuit's petticoat," Jonnie said. She spat down on him and nudged Keke with her heels, turning her back down the hallway. "Would you ride with me there too, Bess? I swear to Her and every soul in her troop, I'll find Sol Rowland and let you do with him what you will." Her free hand came up over her shoulder, brushing the loose ends of my hair. "And after that… we might have to go far, to send these limeys home again."

There was something in her voice I'd never heard before, something akin to doubt. After all this—after the blood and fear, after people we'd known all our lives turning on us, dying by our hands—

"They could never have had you," I told the back of her neck as Keke nudged through the flapping kitchen door into open air. "The Rebs. And if they'd gotten you, they wouldn't have kept you. They didn't understand."

They couldn't fathom it in their bones, a girl who prized freedom above all else—who saw that freedom in the movements of strange, otherworldly animals.

"You understand," Jonnie said, the doubt drained away.

Now and then, if I paused to ponder it, I'd known we were growing up, for there was no way around it. I'd rarely pondered what that meant beyond imagining a house we'd keep together, me a version of Ma and Jonnie of Maria, decorating it just so with my most cherished patterns and notions. Perhaps that was what would come... but now I'd seen what it meant for us, the two of us together, in fact and truth: how love's boundaries stretched, what shapes love took when tested, how love became embodied in something bigger than our own two bodies.

There was no question that I'd ride with her to the ends of the Earth or into the fullness of time, whichever found us first. Ada Nuit's corpse road or the highway north, there was nowhere for me but by her side.

THE END

ABOUT THE AUTHOR

*D*EE HOLLOWAY IS A librarian, writer, and Floridian in upstate New York. Bouncing between romance, speculative fiction, and essays, her work has appeared from publishers as varied as Neon Hemlock, Invisible Oranges, Ancillary Review of Books, World Weaver Press, and more. Her first chapbook was part of Sword & Kettle's *Cup and Dagger* series, and she co-edited *The Book of Korinethians* for Pink Plastic Press. When not dispensing reference services and story time, she's typically tweeting about coffee and horror at @_deeholloway. Explore recent work at Dee's profile on Chill Subs.

ABOUT

QUEEN OF SWORDS PRESS

*Q*UEEN OF SWORDS IS an independent small press,
specializing in swashbuckling tales of derring-do,
bold new adventures in time and space, mysterious
stories of the occult and arcane and fantastical tales of
people and lands far and near. Visit us online at www.
queenofswordspress.com and sign up for our mailing list
to get notified about upcoming releases and offers. Or
follow us on Facebook at the Queen of Swords Press page
so you don't miss any press news.

If you have a moment, the author would appreciate you
taking the time to leave a review for this book at Goodreads,
your blog or on the site you purchased it from.

Thank you for your assistance and your support of
our authors.

CPSIA information can be obtained
at www.ICGtesting.com
Printed in the USA
JSHW060313140723
44546JS00003B/201

9 798986 754345